GODMONSTER

GODMONSTER is a work of fiction. Names, characters, places, and incidents either are the product of the author's imagination or are used factiously. Any resemblance to actual persons, living or dead, events, or locales is entirely coincidental.

Printed in the United States of America

One

Max's night had started off a lot better. Two hours ago, the blood of a maddened tree giant had not drenched a brand-spanking new pair of calfskin leather boots. Two hours ago, Max had been enjoying a rather lovely steak dinner along with a glass of twelve-year bourbon while third-guessing her decision to wear a skin-tight leather skirt on a fifth date with Julien. Sure, her ass was a knockout in the thing, but the skirt really wasn't ideal for the amount of food she needed to shovel into her mouth. Sitting down, the skirt squeezed her midsection hard enough to make breathing a chore, leaving nearly half of the eighteen-ounce cut of meat on her plate with no place to go.

Though it was probably too soon to know if Julien was going to be a keeper, Max found herself being annoyed by how much the guy talked about himself. He also had this habit of asking a question and then either answering it himself, or showing more interest in whatever alert came through his cell phone rather than listening to Max's response. It was a bummer, but other than that, Julien was nice enough. Sex with him was satisfying, and he seemed to genuinely enjoy her company—even if he was partly distracted by emails and social media.

For dinner, Max had ordered enough to keep her stomach full through the following afternoon.

As a marshal of the southern territories, there might be a two-week stretch between paying gigs and the necessary funds to keep the lights on and a roof over her head. Adding to that, her position was low-ranking and highly competitive, so opportunities for big paydays were a scarcity, and even then, sometimes the bounties weren't so cooperative.

Like tonight.

Kneeling next to the thick trunk of an ancient tree, Max took a moment to reload the Smith and Wesson 500. There were only five bullets remaining. Five chances to end this.

She spared another disgusted glance for her ruined boots. They had been a $300 splurge—a sort of gift to herself for keeping her shit together for as long as she had and also for making rent on time three months in a row. Shaking her head, Max pushed thoughts of the once luxurious calf leather from her mind and closed her eyes, shutting out every other sense as her ears strained to hear sounds deep within the forest. It was her only way to track on this rare moonless and starless night.

Poor Nihilson. Her target was one of many tree giants who had curiously ventured through a dimensional rift and landed in this world with no way home. Rifts were uncommon, unstable, and unpredictable. Capable of opening up anywhere and closing at any time, these one-way portals led to other worlds where many unusual, and sometimes dangerous, creatures roamed. The government was still working on a way to predict the rifts and track what came through, but efforts thus far had yielded little success. Luckily, most creatures that crossed a dimensional boundary were able to blend with local wildlife and coexist with humans. When trouble arose, it typically wasn't enough to justify a government-issued warrant for the offender's capture or termination.

Not much was known about tree giants—or kapre, as they were also called—but the giants were usually friendly and sometimes shy, guilty of only small amounts of mischief, like stealing snacks from the backpacks of unsuspecting tourists. A busy afternoon for a kapre meant hanging out in the tree tops while smoking cigars, curiously observing hikers who crossed its path.

But this kapre had suffered a terrible fate. After managing to get himself bitten by a predatory cryptid long believed extinct, Nihilson contracted an incurable and virulent strain of rabies. The suspected timeline from receiving the bite to his first violent assault only spanned three days, but before being captured, the giant had attacked a total of five hikers, three of whom succumbed to their injuries.

A warrant was issued for the maddened kapre's arrest, but Max had not been one of the three marshals who hauled the giant in to the authorities. At the time, Max was farther south tracking different prey. Still, justice was served and Nihilson was tried and convicted by a jury—not of his peers (because where and how would anyone find twelve of the very elusive cryptids?). People still weren't sure exactly how long the life expectancy of a kapre was, but Nihilson's sentence was to spend the remainder of his existence in a maximum-security facility built especially for the most powerful supernatural lawbreakers. However, in transit to the compound, Nihilson killed several guards and escaped. The alert came through to Max's cell maybe a half hour after the incident, but since her phone resided in a sparkly shoulder bag (she was all fancied up for a dinner date after all) and set to vibrate, Max didn't notice the alert for another hour. So, after profuse and repeated apologies, along with a promise from Julien to doggie bag the remainder of dinner and bring it by her apartment, Max had bailed on their date and traveled by cab to reach the largest and closest state park. Since tree giants were extremely territorial, the logical assumption was that Nihilson would return to what was familiar to him, despite his rabid state of mind.

Turning her focus toward the faint snap of a dried twig, Max rallied her nerves and set off cautiously. Kapre were sneaky creatures and were as mighty as the trees in which they lived. It was likely that Nihilson watched her now, waiting to pounce and rip the bones from her flesh before she could react to save herself. This forest was the giant's home, but thanks to Max, he was also seriously injured. As far as she was concerned, they were dead-even in advantage. Okay, maybe dead-even was a stretch. But Max had called for an assist and hoped backup would arrive soon.

Thirty minutes earlier, when she tried capturing Nihilson alive, the plan turned sour once the giant activated some sort of defensive camouflage, blending so well into the surroundings that he literally became invisible to even Max's heightened eyesight. It was something she definitely hadn't counted on and, at first, she couldn't believe it. But then again, not much was known about the kapre. Home base needed to know about this dangerous capability. And once Max overcame the little problem of surviving the night, she would tell them. Ruined boots, bruised ribs, and possible death were the least of her worries. With invisibility on the table, there was a chance Max wouldn't be able to capture Nihilson without contracting rabies herself.

Damn it, she exclaimed in silent regret. *I was an idiot to come out here alone.*

Rolling her neck to relieve the building tension, Max took a deep breath and stepped out into the open. She was going to meet the bastard head on.

The giant took the bait and was on top of her in seconds. A torrent of wind tangled Max's hair and whipped at her eyes as the wake of Nihilson's tremendous power forced her to take a step back. Dropping to her knees, Max tucked and rolled. As a second blast of wind tore at her body, she sprang to her feet and dove in the opposite direction. Biting back a cry as the maneuver punished her already badly damaged ribs, she closed both eyes and focused her senses, hoping her ears could sense what her eyes could not.

There.

Max didn't hesitate. Tracking by sound, she raised the revolver and squeezed the trigger twice to launch fifty caliber bullets into the darkness. That amount of firepower was enough to stop a charging grizzly. Sure, tree giants were a bit larger, but the creatures were also much more docile. When Nihilson roared, she knew at least one bullet had found its target. Grinning, Max opened her eyes and saw too late a glowing stream of blood moving rapidly toward her.

The cloaking ability obviously did not extend to the creature's interior bits. Bright red blood almost glowed in the darkness as it spilled out like a macabre waterfall, pouring from the kapre and onto Max.

Shit. He wasn't down. Those bear-stopping bullets had only managed to piss the giant off more.

Ragged claws tore at her clothing, while from above, hot blood splattered into Max's eyes, dripping into her mouth and nose. She shrieked when the pain of hot knives sliced into her stomach, but Max fought back with everything she had and pumped the remaining bullets into the giant. Nihilson bellowed but did not relent the fury of his attack. Lashing out with the empty revolver, Max screamed when a vise of agony swallowed her forearm. Horrified that the kapre's fangs were injecting the horrible disease into her body, she struck with the opposite fist and fueled every shred of pain she felt into the blow. Again and again, she pummeled the giant, until at last the wicked jaws loosened.

Drenching her hands within the copious spillage of kapre blood, Max smeared the hot liquid against the invisible mass, effectively branding that which sought to destroy her. Then she rocked the giant forward, rolling onto her back as she used Nihilson's own strength and the power in her legs to launch him overhead. Even as his body crashed into the dirt, Max jumped to her feet and scurried to put several feet of space between them.

Her clothing and skin were drenched. Most of the blood was kapre, but some was also hers.

Spitting a mouthful of the acidic-tasting fluid onto the forest floor, Max wiped her lips. The good thing was fluorescent blood now clearly marked the giant, effectively cancelling out his unique camouflage. "There you are," Max whispered.

Too bad she was out of bullets.

Recovering to its full height, the twelve-foot giant charged once more, shaking the ground with each thunderous step. Max readied herself, lowering her center of gravity while keeping her muscles tense. When Nihilson was nearly on top of her, she was ready. Lunging to the right and spinning as she jumped into the air, Max slammed her feet down against the giant's thick hide. The hit was enough to stagger the weakened kapre, but not enough to fell him. Landing two quick snap kicks, she targeted the knees, chopping the giant down to her level. Shifting her weight to one leg, she drove the other foot from the hip, powering her boot into Nihilson's neck, and at last, the kapre collapsed. Shimmering into full view as the insidious camouflage ultimately failed, the massive creature lay at Max's feet, unmoving and struggling to breathe. Max couldn't help feeling pleased with herself. Though she was much stronger than any normal human being, defeating a kapre was no easy task, usually requiring a team effort from two or more marshals.

Slipping on a pair of leather gloves, she withdrew a set of specialized handcuffs from her back pocket. The restraints were of Max's own design. Adjustable to accommodate even the burliest of detainees and lined with hemlock-tipped spikes, struggles from a prisoner only resulted in heavy bleeding and a generous dose of the paralytic compound. Stooping next to the kapre, Max intended to snap the cuffs around his thick wrists, but got a surprise instead. Striking out with one enormous paw, the giant clubbed Max right in the temple. She felt her feet leave the forest floor, but for several frightening seconds, she saw only darkness. Had she been human, the blow would have killed her.

Stunned, Max caged her panic to assess the gravity of the situation. She was face down in the dirt, and her body was riddled with pain. Her skull felt like it had been split apart with a sledgehammer. Gritting her teeth, she rolled her head to one side and forced her eyes open, struggling to focus through a haze of severely blurred vision. She didn't see Nihilson anywhere. Switching tactics, Max concentrated on the tremble in the earth beneath her while listening intently, desperate to feel or hear any trace of the giant.

There.

Just to her left came a series of heavy, rasping breaths. The giant stood maybe a foot away, much too close for her to attempt anything that wasn't foolhardy.

If Max hadn't been on a date when she got the mandate to retrieve the fugitive tree giant, she would have come equipped with a bag full of ammo and firearms, as well as a few knives. In haste, she had left without retrieving extra gear from her apartment, opting instead to come straight from dinner to the national park. Max had hoped a hunting revolver and a pocketful of bullets was enough to bring Nihilson down. Now as the giant's breathing grew louder and his feet scrubbed the earth, bringing him closer to her position, Max realized her thinking had been a serious miscalculation.

Unleashing a roar powerful enough to shake the surrounding foliage, the giant swiped at her motionless body. She fought hard not to recoil from the pain of his jagged claws shredding the flesh from her back. Max wanted to cry, to scream, but willed herself to remain still, and more importantly, silent. Tree giants—even rabid ones—were herbivores and would not eat flesh. If Nihilson believed her dead, he might retreat, allowing her one last ditch effort to win this fight. Unfortunately, a rabid brain was extremely unpredictable, and Nihilson's retreat from a kill could only be expected under normal circumstances.

Roaring again—apparently, madness had robbed the poor guy of all intelligent speech—the giant grabbed her ankle and began dragging her across the forest ground. *Relax*, Max told herself. *Stay cool and you might not die tonight.*

After what seemed like an infinite stretch of time, the giant stopped. Another monstrous howl ripped through the air and his claws tore at her yet again, rolling Max onto her back. She grimaced as her head struck against the rocky soil. Keeping her limbs limp was a struggle, but somehow Max did so, daring to crack her eyelids open just a fraction. It was enough to see the giant, bleeding and enraged, glowering above her with shining orange eyes.

Blood burbled from his lips with each breath, draining down the giant's chin and throat. More of the creature's blood spilled from multiple wounds across its torso and left leg. Yet, somehow, this thing was still standing. Clearly, Nihilson was an exceptionally tough kapre, and even more dangerous than the warrant for his capture had warned.

Then again, bringing him in was supposed to be a two-man job.

Whatever, Max argued with herself. *I am as good as two men.*

Right. Well, tough girl, let's see if you still feel that way when this is over. If you survive.

Bracing for more pain as Nihilson reached for her, Max waited for the right opening to make her move. It came when the giant grabbed her leg and flung her through the air. She hit the ground roughly but rolled with the momentum, pushing to her hands and knees even before her body slid to a stop. Then she shoved to her feet, trying not to think of how every single part of her body would regret this moment later. She needed to win first.

Taking a wide stance, she pulled the Shrike tomahawk from the scabbard slung between her shoulder blades. Military-grade, with all chrome-moly steel construction and a razor-sharp edge that could puncture walls and punch through body armor, the weapon was a last resort for close quarter combat with a tree giant, but Max was out of options. Her earlier call for backup had obviously gone unanswered. It was all about survival now. Both she and the giant could not walk out of this forest alive.

Looking as pissed as ever, Nihilson scraped a clawed foot at the dirt like an angry bull. Puffing out his damaged and bloodied chest, he unleashed another furious growl.

Max wiped a smear of blood from the corner of her mouth. "Well, come and get me, asshole."

Nihilson acquiesced, charging forward like a locomotive from hell. He had plenty of fight left in him. Maybe even more than Max.

As she readied to meet his charge, the unexpected happened. A cannon ball of fire slammed into the creature with explosive force, singeing Max's eyelashes as it knocked Nihilson back ten feet from where the giant once stood. As Nihilson landed unmoving onto the rocky forest floor, Max spun around in disbelief, automatically raising the Shrike to a defensive position. However, the person who emerged from the darkness was unmistakable, and Max lowered her weapon.

Kalista Darkesong. Eternally young and as beautiful as she was dangerous, Kalista was a siren whose abilities were possibly strong enough to match any creature that came through the rifts opening across North America. Thirty years ago, the phenomena hadn't existed. Rumors spoke of a frightening and almost unimaginable event—The Incident—to explain the rifts. After a monstrous beast practically wiped out the entire population of the Americas, a godlike entity was forced to intervene on mankind's behalf. Unfortunately, his efforts to reverse what happened caused the barrier separating Earth from alternate dimensions to deteriorate. Within those alternate worlds resided many dangerous and powerful beings. Not long after "The Incident," those beings began to arrive on Earth. Their presence wasn't noticeable at first as only the tiniest and most harmless sort of creatures wandered over. But as the barrier continued to weaken, larger and more dangerous things were able to cross, making easy prey of a mostly human world. Rumors also claimed that the monstrous beast behind "The Incident" was Kalista's mate. Of course, every government agency—including the one Max worked for—denied the claims, but for some reason, Kalista's husband topped the wanted list for every single one of those agencies.

There were people from an older generation who swore they remembered a separate time line—one where "The Incident" never occurred, and the western hemisphere was never inhabited by monsters seeking to rip humans from their beds in the middle of the night.

Personally, Max wasn't sure what to believe. She had met Kalista's mate, Rhane—aka the monstrous beast—several times. He didn't seem to be nearly as dangerous as his wife, and Max had never witnessed him take anything other than a human form. He was, however, quite skilled with a sword, handled guns extremely well, and was damn near unbeatable in hand-to-hand combat. Rhane was also a total knockout, probably the most gorgeous man Max had ever encountered. One glance into his otherworldly eyes and you just knew the guy was different. Luckily for him, he was brave enough not to hide them.

The marshals were always grateful whenever Rhane showed up to assist with a takedown—it was basically a guaranteed payday—and therefore turned a blind eye to the generous reward offered for his capture. However, money wasn't the only motivator. No one possessed big enough balls or skills to bring Rhane in. And Max definitely wasn't interested in any reward money. Rhane and Kalista were better to have as friends rather than foes.

"Thanks for saving my ass. I didn't expect it to be you," she said as Kalista neared her position. "Not that I don't appreciate it," Max added hastily.

"Were you expecting my husband?"

Max couldn't stop the blush from creeping to her cheeks. Good thing it was dark. A siren's vision wouldn't be as good in the dark. At least Max hoped not. Sure, Rhane was gorgeous, but the guy was also married. She had never entertained a wanton thought where he was concerned. There really was nothing accusatory in Kalista's statement, no inflection at all, in fact. Max simply wasn't used to such directness from the seasoned warrior—a woman who had been hardened by so many battles and subsequently held small talk with little esteem. This was only her second encounter with the siren and, quite simply, Max was a little terrified of her.

Shrugging through the awkwardness, she fumbled with her ruined sweater. "Yeah, but only because Rhane has assisted the marshals several times in the past with these bigger bounties. And he's been a huge help."

Kalista's expression remained unreadable. "Rhane was called away to a different matter."

"Of course." Pinching her lips together, Max avoided uttering anything foolish. Kalista was so intense. For a second, Max stupidly wondered if sirens actually blinked and nearly laughed at the silliness of such a thought. Biting down on her jaw stilled the urge. She couldn't think of a single thing more inappropriate than laughing at that moment.

Finally, Kalista did blink. Slowly scanning Max from head to toe, the siren's gaze hardened. "You're hurt," she said and moved closer, grabbing Max's arm before she could even think of reacting. "Did the kapre's bite break the skin?"

Max gently pulled away. She wanted her arm back, but she also didn't want to offend Kalista. By simply thinking it, a siren could create and control fire, easily doing to Max what she had just done to Nihilson…or worse. "No. I don't think so."

"You should be sure."

"I will," Max assured her before taking a step backward. Sensing something was terribly wrong, she made a slight turn away from Kalista and had about a split second to note the empty ground where the fallen giant once lay. Max felt the rush of wind against her cheek, and then her face was slamming against Kalista's head as their bodies collided, thrown together by a brutal force. Disentangling herself from Kalista, Max recovered the Shrike that had slipped from her grip, thinking it was fool's luck that neither of them landed on the damn thing. She never had time for a second thought because Kalista was literally floating next to Max with a murderous look in her now black and pupil-less eyes. Grey fire surrounded them both, roaring in Max's ears as a whirlwind of flames suddenly exploded outward, scorching the earth and trees in its wake. When the fire dissipated, somehow Nihilson still stood, but the entirety of his nine-foot silhouette was entirely engulfed.

Kalista moved toward the giant, rage blazing from her eyes as she raised her arms and intensified the fire. Nihilson roared, but his fight was done. The giant crashed to his knees with the stench of burnt flesh choking the air. Flames bore down on him continuously, consuming his already blackened carcass to melt away skin, fat, muscle and bone. At last, only ashes were left. Then night became dark once more as Kalista finally extinguished her flames.

It took a while for Max to find her voice. "Wow," she whispered, gazing at Kalista in complete awe. "When I grow up, I want to be like you."

Kalista wiped a trickle of blood from the corner of her mouth. She still looked pretty pissed. "Sorry about your bounty."

Shrugging, Max walked over to the pile of remains and kicked through the ashes, trying not to think of how much more ruined her boots would be once blood mixed in with tree giant dust. When her toe hit something solid, Max stooped down. It only took a few passes to find them—one full set of kapre teeth. Smiling, she showed Kalista her prize. Only three of the enormous molars could fit into her palm at one time.

"A live capture would have been much better. I won't get as much, but proof of death will be worth something."

Kalista nodded. "This is why they don't send me, you know. I lose my temper."

Max studied Nihilson's remains, already being scattered by the chilly mountain breeze, and decided to never ever anger a siren.

Two

Morning came way too fast. After filling two evidence bags with teeth—all that remained of Nihilson—Max had returned to her apartment and promptly collapsed into bed, snoozing for several hours. Not tired, but far from refreshed, she woke up and checked her phone, squinting to make sure her eyes had read the screen correctly. Nearly a dozen missed calls, and all were from the same number. *Great*. Max groaned. There'd be hell to pay later.

Rolling to the side of the bed, she used her cell to text a brief message, reporting Nihilson's termination to the company, but she would actually have to take the bag of teeth to the office in order to procure payment.

Max rubbed her eyes. The sandpaper feel wasn't going anywhere until she removed the contacts she'd slept in all night. Tugging off her ruined boots, Max was dismayed to find them in even worse shape than she thought. Tossing her skirt and blouse aside, she let them land wherever they fell. Sunday was laundry day. She would tidy up then. The long wig of shiny and straight black hair was next to come off, allowing Max's unruly mass of golden spirals to tumble over her shoulders.

Completely naked except for a tiny, hot pink thong, Max headed to the bathroom sink to deal with the gritty contacts. There was nothing wrong with her vision. It was better than 20/10. The lenses were simply to give her eyes a more socially acceptable appearance, allowing her to blend in with humankind without freaking out every person who crossed her path. The wig served the same purpose. Max's skin was far too dark for blond hair or golden eyes to look even remotely normal.

Starting with the left lens, she was super careful with its removal. Overnight, her fingernails had grown absurdly long and thick— just like they always did. Max typically waited until after breakfast to trim them, but she also didn't usually pass out like a drunken college girl and sleep until almost noon.

The dark brown contacts hid irises that were amber-flaked and just as golden as her hair, plus were great camouflage for the one vertically-slit pupil. In her natural state, Max was cautious to never linger in front of mirrors. So, after hurriedly brushing her teeth, she started the shower. It wasn't that Max was ashamed of what she was. No. Max just didn't *know* what she was. Long before she was born, her father had volunteered for a series of mostly successful experiments funded by a private security sector seeking to produce a more elite soldier. Her father, however, still looked like a normal guy, requiring no complicated disguise to blend in. By all standards, Max Sr. was human—just a better version of one. Max figured her dad must have stuck his dick in something pretty weird in order to produce offspring like her. Strangely though, her mother was a mystery he refused to reveal. For the entirety of her life, Max had gone without knowing the woman who had given birth to her. She had never even seen a picture. So, whenever Max stared into a mirror, she thought of who or what her mother might be, and from there it was a hard fight not to become consumed with searching for her again.

Ten years ago, when Max was still a teenager, she had attempted to discover her mother's identity. Her father found out and became about as angry as Max had ever seen him. After confiscating her computer and journal, he had taken her by shoulders, physically shaking his daughter as he forbade her to ever attempt something so stupid again. But it wasn't her father's anger that stopped Max from searching. Instead, it was the fear in his eyes that made her obey his wishes.

On the bright side, Max's odd appearance was accompanied with other more useful gifts. Her high tolerance for pain came in handy each time she took on an oversized and dangerous predator. She also possessed a heightened sense of hearing, remarkable agility, and superhuman strength that equaled just about any enhanced soldier who crossed her path. Max healed much faster than a regular human. Inspecting her torso as she stepped from the shower, Max examined the injuries she'd sustained last night, now only ugly, but healing, yellow bruises. Across her back and shoulders, even the angry slashes of Nihilson's claws had crusted over. Her body was sore as shit though.

Toweling dry, she shimmed into a more comfortable thong and a pair of yoga pants. While slipping an oversized black dolman overhead, a succession of furious knocks pounded at the apartment door, causing Max to nearly jump out of her skin. At first bewildered by who it could be, she then froze. Julien had promised to bring the leftovers from dinner by her apartment. He couldn't see her like this. The crazy golden hair would be forgivable, but nothing else. Her eyes were much too dry to tolerate even a fresh pair of contacts, and she had yet to trim the thick, talon-like nails. Feeling guilty as hell, Max ignored the knocking. But then a key slipped into the lock, and she froze.

Two seconds later, her ex-boyfriend stormed into the apartment wearing the countenance of an angry pit viper. Harrison Preesti. Six feet and five inches of moodiness, arrogance, and a bull-headed mindset, Priest was a self-proclaimed asshole who could also be the most charming, loving, and loyal companion a girl could ask for. He was and probably always would be the one guy Max could never shake.

Crossing the room in a few powerful strides, his savage blue eyes glared down at her like a pair of radioactive sapphires as he spoke. "If you're not going to answer your phone, you may as well throw it into the goddamn ocean."

Max crossed her arms. "I never gave you a key to this place. What are you doing here?"

Priest's scowl deepened. "You didn't return my calls."

"I didn't want to talk to you."

Beneath the sun-kissed complexion, every blood vessel in Priest's face expanded, sending a flood of crimson that stretched from the bottom of his tensely wrought jaw to the edge of his hairline. Even when angry, Priest was an attractive guy. Genetic engineering at its finest. His features were probably too rugged to model men's fashion, but he could definitely pass for the kind of actor who was a shoo-in to be the next action star on the big screen. In real life, Priest was a sort of action hero. Aside from a secondary role as her father's errand boy, he saw plenty of action in his line of work. He was team leader of an elite kill squad tasked to hunt the deadliest creatures that entered through any rift. If his team was sent after a target, it was because the government had deemed it too dangerous for capture. His presence indicated whomever or whatever he was hunting was as good as dead, earning him the moniker "Priest" because it was time for last rites.

Naturally platinum blond in color, his hair was perfectly coiffed, buzzed at the sides but rather longish on top. The trendy style starkly contrasted the utilitarian manner in which he dressed...mostly in all black. People often underestimated Priest, errantly assuming his beauty and brawn was backed by neither brains or skill. Watching him prove them wrong time and time again never got old. Secretly, Max thought Priest became even hotter when he was angry. Maybe it was why she not-so-secretly enjoyed pissing him off.

"That's real mature, Maximum," he said, finally replying to the reason she'd given for not answering any of his dozen calls.

"Don't call me that." It was Max's turn to be annoyed. Maximum had always been her father's nickname for her. Back when they were dating, Priest had used it on occasion, and that was okay. But not anymore. Not after what he did.

Max chewed her lip. "How's my dad?"

Priest softened a little. He was quite familiar with the turbulence between Max and her father. "He's good. Misses you."

"Where is he this time?" She knew he wouldn't answer but pressed her luck anyway.

"I can't tell you that. You know better."

"Damn it, Priest."

"I'm just the messenger."

"Well, message delivered. You can leave now."

His frown returned. "That's not why I came."

Max let out an exasperated sigh. "Do we really have to do this?"

"You know the deal. If you don't answer, I come looking."

"Ohmygod, Priest. I'm a big girl. I can take care of myself. The fact that I've been doing so all these years should be proof enough. You and my father need to lay off."

"This isn't just him, Max. That bounty you went after *alone* was at least a two-marshal job. When you didn't report to confirm kill or capture, I didn't know what to think."

For the first time, Max paid closer attention to the scruff of reddish-blond beard shadowing Priest's normally fresh-shaven face and the dark splotches beneath both eyes. He must have lost a few night's worth of sleep because one night of worrying wouldn't have affected him so drastically. Something else had to be going on. Perusing multiple suspicions in her mind, Max relented. "I should have reported in sooner."

For a second, Priest actually looked surprised. Then he dropped his head, moved closer and brought his hands to rest atop her shoulders. "I'm glad you're okay."

"Thanks," Max said and slid out of reach. The heat from his touch was too much. Seeing a spark light within his eyes, she realized dodging him had been a mistake.

Closing the distance again, he positioned himself so that their bodies were within centimeters of touching. "Did I make you nervous just then?"

"No," she answered stiffly. But her heart was already beating faster and Priest would have certainly heard. The smirk on his face pretty much confirmed he had.

Bending so his head was next to hers, he whispered, "Maxima Masters, I think you're lying to me."

Another knock sounded at the door, making her jump about a foot into the air. *Shit.* This time it really had to be Julien, bringing the leftovers from last night. She looked at Priest with pleading eyes. "Please don't do anything."

A big, stupid smile spread across his face. "You're real popular this morning," he said and sniffed the air. The mischief in his gaze threatened to send Max into a panic attack. "I don't think I've met this one."

"Priest," she said firmly, willing to do whatever was necessary to stop what was about to happen. "I am sorry for not returning your calls. I will answer the next time. I swear it."

Trailing a finger down her forearm, Priest shook his head. "I think you're lying again, Maximum."

Behind them, Julien's knocking had resumed. "Damn it," Max said and made a quick dash for the bathroom. Her eyes may have been too sore for contacts but sunglasses would do. She'd just pretend to be hung over. Her wig was nearby, gloves would hide the fingernails and—Priest's arms enfolded about her waist, lifting Max up as if she weighed as much as a feather and carried her back to the living room.

"Priest, cut it out," she ordered, struggling against him.

"It's open," he called to Max's absolute horror. "Come on in."

"You asshole," she hissed. Priest wasn't going to let go unless she made him. Driving one elbow backward, she aimed for his face but he easily blocked the blow. Max had anticipated that, needing him to take one hand away from her body in order to protect himself, so she could attack the opposite. Grabbing the pinky of the hand still holding her, she twisted it backward.

It worked. Priest swore and let go, abruptly setting her feet back on the floor. Just as Julien

27

entered, Max spun away so he wouldn't see her face. Pulse thundering in her ears, she almost didn't hear when he said her name.

"Max?" His voice was thick with confusion.

Fisting her hands to hide the ghastly fingernails, she forced herself to be calm. Nervously clearing her throat, she summoned a smile even though Julien couldn't see it, and forced a lightness into her tone. "Hey, Julien."

"So, that is you." His footsteps came closer. They sounded hesitant, but at least some of the tension left his speech. "I didn't know you were a blonde."

Shit. Shit. Shit. Shit.

Max seriously regretted not breaking Priest's finger. "Yeah," she said, trying to keep her voice light. "I like to play around with new hairstyles, but I guess I'm too chicken to actually commit."

Priest uttered something between a laugh and a cough. "You can say that again."

And his nose. She should have broken his nose.

"Who is this guy?" Julien asked, his tone taking on a protective note. "Is he hassling you?"

Uh oh. Max was out of time. Priest wasn't the type of guy to go around starting fights, but she had never known him to back down from one either. He was a weapon by design and genetically engineered to have heightened aggression. If Julien confronted her ex, Priest would destroy him.

Resigning to her fate, Max slowly turned to face Julien. The fallout was instant. One glance at her circus-freak eye and fear erased every good thing Julien had ever thought about her. Dressed in a dark suit with no tie—his idea of Saturday casual—he took a huge step backward. "Oh my God, what happened to you?"

"It's okay," she said quickly, raising her hand to reassure him that everything was fine but that was exactly the wrong move. Julien's stunned expression locked onto the three-inch claws protruding from her nailbeds, and Max steeled her heart for what would follow.

"N-never mind," Julien stammered. "I'll call you later," he promised. Stumbling over his own feet as he rushed to leave the apartment, he tossed the bag of leftovers over his shoulder just before slamming the door behind him.

Blinking back a single tear, Max watched him go. No matter how many times it happened, rejection never hurt any less.

"Are you happy now?" she whispered.

"No. He almost had me convinced when he stuck up for you, but then one glimpse at the real you and he ran out of here like a scared little princess. I'm sorry, Max." Stepping in front of her, Priest trailed one finger across her jaw. "Don't hide yourself for people like that."

Rage flared in her chest, overtaking the pain, and Max could only see red. Without thinking, she lashed out and struck Priest across the face. Staggered by either surprise or the force of the blow, Priest touched his cheek where four slashes now trickled blood.

"How dare you?" she said, her voice low and seething.

Priest's eyes darkened dangerously. "Did it feel good to hit me?" Whipping his head forward in a blur, he stopped just before their noses touched. "Do it again, Max. Hit me."

Unable to stand the way he saw through her, Max shut her eyes.

Priest's hand immediately closed around her throat. "Don't look away from me."

She gritted her teeth. She could already feel her body beginning to betray her, responding to him as it always did.

His hand squeezed tighter. "Look at me," he said in a soft whisper.

Slowly, Max relented and saw exactly what she feared. Enough heat radiated from his gaze to knock her over. She responded by slapping his other cheek.

Priest barely flinched.

"I hate you," she nearly spat.

"No you don't," he said, and crushed his mouth against hers.

Between the kiss and the hand squeezing her throat, Max could hardly contain her growing excitement. Barely able to breathe, she matched Priest's eagerness, tasting every sweet part of his mouth as his tongue caressed hers. She sucked him deeper, not ever wanting the kiss to stop, but suddenly, Priest released her and air flooded her lungs, leaving Max lightheaded. Priest's chest heaved as he breathed, but otherwise he didn't move. The message was clear. Whatever happened next was up to her.

"Damn you," she whispered and reached for him. He met her halfway, and their bodies crashed together. Priest's hands were everywhere at once, sliding through the mess of her hair, fondling her ass and squeezing her breasts. Against her belly, his arousal thickened and pressed insistently into her. Sliding her hand down the hardening bulge, she grabbed his shaft roughly, and Priest stiffened, thrusting his hips forward, moving one hand to her throat again. He moaned as she squeezed him, and his cock jerked between her fingers, becoming engorged beneath her encouraging strokes.

A low growl slid from his lips just before he tossed her through the air and onto the couch. Pouncing on top of her, he stripped away her yoga pants, leaving Max naked from the waist down. Clouded by lust, his gaze settled on the thin strip of pubic hair, a vertical runway to her sweet spot.

"Was that for him?"

"Well, he was my boyfriend," she said, wanting to get under his skin. "Julien only liked to do it in the bedroom though. Big fan of reverse cowgirl," she purred.

That purr became a moan as two of Priest's fingers plunged inside of her. Then his thumb pressed against her clit, starting a swirl of maddening circles. Soon, Max was shuddering beneath his skillful touch.

"I know what you like, Maximum." His fingers pushed deeper, slowly thrusting in and out, sliding through the stream of wetness he coaxed from her body, as he watched her with hungry, glittering eyes. Sweat beaded across Max's skin. Her body tightened. His thumb circled harder and the fingers inside of her curled inward. Biting her lip, she threw her head back and broke apart, succumbing to the pleasure of spasms that racked her body. Every muscle seized up, curling her legs around Priest, locking him between her shaking thighs. And then Max collapsed, panting and hungry for more.

Priest took off his shirt, exposing a chiseled chest and washboard abs. His entire torso was covered by tattoos—shades of black and grey ink camouflaging scars earned from battle and the remnants of abuse from the hands of overzealous scientists conducting experiments to determine his limits. Priest was the product of a morally questionable program that was doomed for failure from the onset. Out of thousands of embryos grown within a Global Cures lab, only a few hundred were allowed to leave their tubes and breathe air. A programing stage came next, and in less than six months, the embryos were an army of fully matured adults—perfect soldiers, specifically created to fight whatever threat rose up against the power that controlled them. Less than a decade into the program, a fatal flaw in "Project Washington" was revealed, and all of its subjects—except for a lucky handful—were terminated. As one of Project Washington's few survivors, Priest was the definition of a warrior, and had transformed his body into a canvas depicting a war between all things good and evil.

Reaching up, Max touched where a serrated blade had plunged into his ribs almost three years ago. A dragon now masked the scar, curling around a broadsword as it breathed fire at its enemies. Punishment only made Priest mentally and physically stronger. She had always admired that about him. When things had ended so horribly with Priest, Max had spiraled into a pattern of self-destructive behavior, becoming mired in a tunnel of resentment and anger that no light could pierce through. It had taken the love and enduring patience of close friends to pull her off that dark path. She hadn't realized how much she cared for Priest until being with him was no longer an option.

"Hey," Priest said softly, dragging her away from painful memories. "You think too much."

"One of us has to."

Pushing her hair back, he lowered his lips to her neck and planted a series of kisses in her most sensitive areas. More than ten months had passed since they'd been this intimate, but he clearly remembered her body well. Digging her nails into his powerful biceps, Max moaned and writhed beneath the passionate assault.

"If you don't want this to happen," he whispered between kisses, "tell me to stop and I will."

Gritting her teeth, Max clung to him, trying and failing to pull back from the lust. She needed to place her feet on the solid ground of reason and good sense. She needed to stop this. But then his fingers slid between her thighs once more, pushing oh so sweetly inside of her, and any thought of resistance faded. Gasping, Max dug her nails into his back.

Priest groaned. "You're so wet. Stop being stubborn and tell me you want me."

Max could barely think through the haze of desire but opened her mouth anyway, knowing full well she would regret her words. At the same time, Priest's hands slid against her stomach as he pushed the oversized shirt up past her hips. A second later, every kelvin of heat fled his expression, chilling his face into a block of solid ice.

"Goddammit, Max."

Three

It took a full three seconds for Max's brain to catch up. *Oops*. Though her injuries had almost healed, her body still looked pretty banged up. Up until now, clothing had hidden the evidence of exactly how close she'd come to losing the fight against the tree giant, but now her carelessness had been exposed. And oh boy, was Priest pissed.

Shoving his hands away, Max pulled her shirt down to cover her battered skin and stood from the couch, avoiding eye contact as she plucked her thong and yoga pants from the floor, quickly shimmying them up over her hips. There was no way she was getting laid at this point, and Max couldn't be half-naked while hashing things out with Priest. From the look in his eye, he was gearing up to deliver a verbal lashing fit for the record books.

"I thought you were done taking insane risks," he said quietly, but his anger boiled over into every syllable.

Max still didn't look at him. The fury in his voice told her everything she needed to know. His chest would heave as he tried to stay calm long enough to get his point across before the unproductive screaming match began.

"Last night was no riskier than any other." Turning away, Max picked up the doggie bag Julien had tossed aside and stashed it in the refrigerator. The steak would be great for dinner. Right now, breakfast was the mystery to solve.

"Those bruises say the opposite. I read the warrant, Max. The tree giant you went after had contracted an incurable strain of rabies. You're lucky you weren't bitten."

Oh he bit me alright. It just didn't break the skin. Keeping that little detail to herself, she redirected her search to the cupboards. "I got the call while I was having a lovely date with Julien, so I didn't have all my gear—just the Smith & Wesson, some fifty-cal ammo, and my trusty tomahawk." Max shrugged like it was no big deal. "That revolver can take down a bear, so I figured it would be more than enough."

"Well, you figured wrong."

Finding nothing on the shelves safely within the suggested expiration dates, Max closed the cabinet doors. *Damn.* She drummed the fingers of one hand against the countertop while contemplating her options, and risked a fleeting glance at Priest. Still shirtless, his perfect abs and rippling muscles made him a poster child for genetic engineering. Though he was a handsome guy, he was also dangerous. For some reason, Max kept forgetting that. At least he actually looked pretty calm—except for the one vein pulsating at the side of his neck.

"You're right," she admitted, folding her arms. "I totally underestimated the shit storm I was rushing into. It turns out that kapre have a very unique ability to camouflage themselves."

Priest's anger was briefly tempered by surprise. "What, like shifters?"

"No, like *invisibility*. I couldn't see him, Priest. The bastard just disappeared."

"Max—" he began, but she quickly interrupted.

"I know. I know. It was a crazy risk, but Nihilson was worth a lot of money. I couldn't let his warrant go to another marshal. And I did call for backup, Priest. She was just a little late getting there."

"If backup is late, then you wait. You don't go charging in half-cocked."

"Well you would know all about that, wouldn't you," Max muttered.

"Excuse me?" Priest leaned across the counter. The vein was really throbbing now. "I always wait for my team."

Max scoffed. "Oh that's right. You are always such a team player. Total boy scout. That's you. If Sir says "jump," Priest doesn't need to know how high to jump or who he's going to hurt. He just leaps over the fucking moon."

Priest's jaw clenched down tight enough to break a couple of teeth. Max waited. She knew she had touched a nerve.

Taking a deep breath, he finally spoke. "Max, I just want you to be more careful."

"I'll agree to be more careful if you agree to be less of an asshole."

He raised one eyebrow. "Are you seriously mad about Jamal?"

"His name is Julien," she spat. "Did it ever occur to you to *not* barge into my home uninvited, humiliate me, and scare off my boyfriend? You're un-fucking-believable."

Sighing, Priest didn't speak for a while. "Okay. That's fair," he finally said. "I'm sorry about Ja—Julien." Lifting both hands from the counter, he made a placating gesture. "I've seen playhouses with more real food in them. Let me buy you breakfast and make it up to you."

Max blinked at him. Considering their history, the argument had never really started. Priest was conceding before things even escalated into a full-blown war. She couldn't believe it. Still, Max wasn't swayed. "Thanks," she said icily, "but buying me breakfast at your favorite shitty diner isn't going to make up for what you did. Besides, I've got everything under control here."

Mentally crossing her fingers, she went back to the fridge, this time aiming for the freezer drawer at the bottom. Max smiled triumphantly on finding a lone package of frozen whole wheat waffles. There were three left inside the box. One looked kinda gross and freezer-burned—she would offer that one to Priest—but the other two were fine. Popping the yucky waffle and a fresh one into the toaster, Max grabbed two glasses and filled them with tap water from the sink. After a beat of hesitation, she handed one to Priest thinking if he was going to play nice, she would go along with the cease fire.

A somewhat awkward silence hung between them until the toaster ejected the waffles. Max kept one for herself and tossed Priest the soggy one, which he easily caught. She pushed the remaining waffle down into the toaster.

Grinning, Max munched on her breakfast and watched as Priest suspiciously eyed the waffle that was already falling apart in his huge hands. Taking an uncertain bite, he frowned and threw the rest in the trash. "It's disturbing how you're able to eat that. Let's go get some real food, and it doesn't have to be at my favorite shitty diner. You pick the place."

Max collected the second waffle, spreading a little peanut butter and jam across the surface. "Can't," she said between mouthfuls. "I have to go to the agency and turn in proof of death in order to collect payment. How about a raincheck?"

Looking hopeful and disappointed all at once, he shrugged his chiseled shoulders. "Only if you mean it."

"I won't make any promises."

"Right," Priest replied curtly as his face closed off from further emotion. Without another word, he grabbed his shirt and strapped on a gun Max had not even noticed. No surprise there. Priest carried everywhere he went.

Retreating into her bedroom, she snagged a lightly worn sports bra from the overflowing laundry basket in the corner. From her peripheral, she saw Priest's large form fill the doorway. Of course he would follow her. Turning around, Max looked him straight in the eye as she removed her shirt, exposing her full breasts along with every bruise, scratch, and scrape from last night's battleground.

Expression darkening, Priest crossed the room and took her chin in one hand. "One day you will have to forgive me," he said in a voice softened by regret. "I thought I was protecting you, Maxima."

Her brain stalled. The comment had thrown Max off guard because she and Priest didn't talk about what happened. It hurt too much on both sides. Maybe that was the problem. The sudden rawness at the back of her throat made it difficult to swallow. *That's what happens when you blindly follow orders. Even ones dictated by my father.* "Thanks for the orgasm," she said out loud, and briskly pulled on a sweatshirt. "Lock up when you leave." Then Max hurried out of the apartment, slamming the door before the first traitorous tear could fall.

*

The office of the United States Paranormal Marshal Services was located only a few blocks from Max's apartment building. Stopping at the trunk of her car to grab a duffel containing a loosely rolled yoga mat, water bottle, and towel, Max stuffed the evidence bags into the duffel and set out on foot to turn over the proof of kill. She checked her watch. It would be less than an hour before her best friend's Saturday afternoon yoga class started. Max had promised to make an appearance at the struggling fitness studio, so all-encompassing, painful bruises be damned, she planned to keep her word.

USPMS was situated on the thirteenth floor of a fifteen-story building. Nine of the lower floors were open to the public, but to access levels ten and above required special authorization. Stepping onto the elevator, Max swiped her badge to illuminate additional floor selections on the control panel and unlock access to them. Then she selected number thirteen. Lurching to a slow start, the elevator lumbered up twelve stories and dropped her off in the main lobby of the thirteenth floor. Cute Kevin greeted her from behind the expansive front desk surfaced with black marble. His hazel eyes were friendly and bright, and his smile—capable of melting the panties off even a celibate prude—shined even brighter despite having to work the weekend shift. Though Cute Kevin's sexual leanings favored men, he kept an open mind. And that was all any single woman who passed through these doors needed to hear before shamelessly throwing herself at his feet. If the rumors held any truth to them, the ride was well worth the cost of admission. But Max had never felt any attraction toward USPMS's charming receptionist. They'd oftentimes hung out after work at a nearby club, but the only pull she felt toward him was for friendship.

Max waved at Kevin's greeting but kept walking, intending to stroll right past him. Sure, he was a great guy and an even better friend, but he could also be long-winded. And Max was in a hurry.

"Sunglasses indoors? You must be hungover," Kevin said, making a sympathetic face.

Max answered as succinctly as possible. "I'm fine."

Her purposeful steps were forced to halt in front of the double steel doors that barred access to all administrative areas of the thirteenth floor. The doors remained sealed unless an almost self-aware biometric security system granted access.

Max didn't have direct clearance for entry. She and all other marshals were restricted to the exterior regions. But, in addition to being a secretary, Cute Kevin was the gatekeeper and could manually override the doors.

"Love the hair, Max," he said from behind her, ignoring the obvious hint that she did not want to talk. "Sometimes I forget you're a natural goldilocks."

"Thanks," she said, and patted her bun absently. Forced to flee the apartment without wearing one of her wigs, Max had found salvation in an oversized hair-tie. The little black band was currently strained to its limit, struggling to control a frizzy mass of loose curls. Max pointed at the sealed corridor meaningfully. "I need to see the director."

"Yes, of course." Leaning across the desk, Kevin clucked his teeth. "I hear you took down escapee one-two-seven without waiting for an assist. Are you trying to get yourself killed, sweetheart?"

Begrudgingly, Max turned to face him. She really didn't need her friends getting all worked up again about the state of her mental health. "Kevin, I'm in a hurry. I don't have time for you to give me shit about last night too."

Folding both hands beneath his chin, he smiled. "Now who possibly could have already reprimanded you for your suicidal behavior at this hour on a Saturday? Arabella has been at the studio all morning, and I know for a fact that Jensen had a very late night. He was still dancing when I left Gents & Belles."

Max winced. Kevin knew all the gritty details about her life. Most of them she told him voluntarily, but sometimes he sussed things out before getting a full confession. At times, she got the impression that Kevin possessed an uncanny ability to make inferences about strictly private things. But then again, he also had a lot of friends with keen eyes and big mouths.

She huffed a sigh. "Don't do that, Kevin. I hate it when you do that."

"Do what?" he asked, batting his eyelashes innocently.

"Corner me with the threat of knowing intimate information I haven't told you."

Kevin offered a placating smile. "No one is threatening you. And since I didn't mention intimacy either…" Chuckling, he let the sentence trail.

Cheeks growing hot, her mind automatically strayed to exactly how intimate things had gotten with Priest this morning. Max groaned. If Kevin hadn't already known, certainly her blush was as good as an open admission. She tried steering the conversation toward her original purpose for coming to the agency. Maybe he would mercifully drop the subject.

"Is the director in?"

"He is." Leaning back in his chair, Kevin folded both hands behind his head and smiled.

When he said nothing further, Max let out an exasperated breath. "Well, is he busy? Can I see him?"

"Yes, but also yes. He's expecting you to bring in proof of death."

Seriously running thin on patience, Max tried not to bare her teeth. "Well I can't do that unless you buzz me in, Kevin."

Of course, he wasn't going to do so without getting what he wanted first, and because it was Saturday morning, the office was mostly empty. Kevin was free to play his little game of extortion.

"We're getting there, sweetheart. Just hold your horses."

"Ohmygod," Max muttered, but had no choice except to stand there and wait.

"The radiant glow of your skin tells me that you orgasmed this morning, but the way you blushed earlier—now that brings more to the tale. Your pleasure session wasn't solo play. No. No." Wagging his finger, Kevin grinned again. "I like you, Max, so I won't make you say it. Just nod if you spent some quality time with that ruggedly handsome ex-boyfriend of yours this morning."

This time Max did bare her teeth. She also nodded.

Clapping his hands together, Kevin sat up straighter. "There's hope for you two lovebirds yet."

"You must have forgotten why we ended things in the first place," Max replied dryly.

"Oh no. One could never forget that. Priest did a cruel and shitty thing. But from what I gather, what he did was to protect you…in a really twisted, sadistic sort of way," he finished, looking off to the side as his voiced trailed thoughtfully.

"We'll have to agree to disagree on that one."

"And so we shall."

Max took a calming breath. "Kevin," she said as sweetly as she could.

"Patience really isn't your strong suit, is it, Max?"

"No, it sure isn't," she replied and was relieved to hear the motorized doors begin to open. "That's probably why I always end up with more kills than captures." She directed her most serious stare toward him, but the intent was hidden behind dark sunglasses she had yet to remove.

Kevin nodded gravely. "The same could be said about your love life."

"Ouch," Max said with exaggerated woe, but swiftly retreated into the open corridor before Kevin changed his mind. "These little chats always give me such eye-opening insight into the failures of my personal life. I thank you, Kevin."

He winked. "You're welcome, sweetheart."

Rolling her eyes, Max covered the distance to the director's corner office at a brisk march. Negotiations with Kevin had taken too much time, and now she was going to be hard-pressed to make it to yoga class. Hopefully, the director would settle for a quick summarization of last night's events and wait to receive a full report on Monday morning. She crossed her fingers. *Yeah right.*

"Come in," a deep voice commanded just before she could knock. "Marshal, I've been expecting you."

"Good morning, Sir," Max said as she pushed into the office and inclined her head respectfully. In the three years she'd served as a marshal for the lower seven districts, there had been probably fewer than a dozen exchanges between herself and the regional director, Kevin Cranke. It was for the best. Max had a much healthier relationship with authority when she stayed out of its way. Besides, she found it way more satisfying to be the one giving the orders. Out the field, a marshal was pretty much his or her own boss. Whenever a warrant was issued, the only advisement received was whether to bring the creature in dead or alive. Even then, there was still some flexibility as to *how* alive or dead.

Mr. Cranke, aka Cranky Kevin, greeted her with a warm smile. The director's nickname actually had little to do with his character. For the most part, he was a friendly, approachable guy, but beneath his kind demeanor was a ruthless intelligence that wasn't afraid to do whatever was necessary to get the job done. To some, he was quite intimidating, but Max liked him. She couldn't imagine working for a better guy.

"What's with the sunglasses?" he asked, studying her with a curious gaze.

"Sorry, sir. Pink eye." It was a lame excuse, but it was a better lie than telling her boss or letting him infer that she was hungover. The director, like everyone else in the office, knew Max was different, but they'd erroneously assumed she was another enhanced human, attributing her enhanced abilities to genetic tampering and elite training. None of them had never seen Max in her freakish natural state, and she wasn't ready to change that.

The director gestured for her to close the door, a sure sign it might not be the short conversation she hoped for. "Sit down," he said. His steely eyes, surrounded by a pair of black-rimmed frames, sparkled with amusement. "I've heard quite the rumor about your handling of the fugitive tree giant. Your call for backup was recorded, but no other agents have reported an assist. You're a very formidable agent, and I've never doubted your skills, but all morning I have found myself pondering how it was that you were able to bring down a maddened kapre alone."

Max took a seat in one of two cushy, conference-style chairs situated before the director's desk. "To be honest, I wondered the same thing. Last night Nihilson revealed an ability that wasn't in his file. I had the giant cornered and badly wounded when he disappeared."

Director Cranke raised one eyebrow. "Disappeared?"

"Yeah. He had this sort of natural camouflage that made him blend perfectly into his surroundings, like a chameleon on steroids."

"Well that's rather concerning. And despite this, you were able to subdue this creature alone?"

Max considered her reply carefully. Though she liked and respected the director, she couldn't tell him about Kalista's role in bringing down Nihilson. Kalista's mate was a wanted man, pursued by government agencies all around the world. A hefty reward came with his capture, and Max saw no reason to dangle such a tempting carrot in front of the director. There was no doubt, of course, that Cranke already knew about his subordinates' secret dealings with Rhane and how they turned a blind eye to his criminal status. Suspicion and blatant admission, however, were two very different things. Max wasn't about to confess to aiding or abetting.

She nodded. "I got lucky. Really lucky."

"Did you bring proof of the kill?" Director Cranke asked, indicating he was—at least for now—willing to accept that simple explanation.

"I did." Max reached into her gym bag. Extracting the kapre teeth, she placed them into Cranke's outstretched hand.

He shook his head. "Poor bastard."

"Yeah."

The director appeared to lose himself in thought for a quiet moment while examining the remains. Max waited patiently, hoping he wouldn't press for more details. Cranke was a good guy, and she hated lying to him.

Heaving a deep sigh, he stood from the desk. Even on weekends, the director dressed for his elevated role. It was a shame really. Cranky Kevin's face wasn't all that attractive, but he definitely had a nice body. Max would have loved to see his tight ass in a pair of jeans just once. But today, like always, she'd have to settle for well-tailored dress slacks.

"That'll be all, Masters. Expect the funds to be transferred to your account on Monday."

"Thank you, sir."

"Oh, and Masters," he said, stopping her as she turned to leave the office. "On Monday, also expect to deliver a report detailing every moment of this kapre kill. Be as specific as you can regarding the new ability you witnessed. And I want that report first thing. We need to get this information on record."

"Yes sir." Max smiled tightly. The report would have to be less than truthful, but at least she wouldn't have to lie her ass off during a face-to-face interview with someone she respected.

"Great. I'll see you at the gala tonight, marshal."

"Yes, sir. See you tonight."

Four

Hastily exiting the sequestered offices, Max was relieved to see that Cute Kevin had stepped away from the reception desk. She bolted across the empty lobby before he could return, but had to stop for the elevator and stood shifting her weight, nervously counting the seconds until the doors opened. Max didn't relax until she was inside the elevator and safely in motion.

She checked her watch. The yoga studio was only ten blocks away. If Max hurried, she would make it to class almost on time. Running at full speed would have gotten her there faster, but attracting too much attention to herself on the busy city streets was a terrible idea. So, Max jogged at a human pace, enduring the annoyance of a pair of sneakers in her gym bag that jarred against her butt with every step. Reaching the complex—home of a fitness gym and a seedy law firm—she threw open the opaque glass door and took the stairs three at a time. Skittering onto the second story landing, Max dashed through the studio entrance, barely stopping to scribble her name on the sign-in sheet and slowed only as she entered class. Smoothing her hair, she adjusted it, pulling the bun tighter, and then unrolled her mat to claim an open spot at the back.

Busy leading the group of fourteen—now fifteen—women and two men into a series of downward dog stretches, was Max's former roommate and best friend, Arabella. Graced with silky, strawberry-blonde hair, clear green eyes, impeccable skin, and the body of a goddess, Arabella was a model of perfection, the embodiment of the most elite reproductive sciences. Literally, Arabella's face graced the cover of every clinic brochure.

Catching Max's eye, Arabella frowned disapprovingly before breaking into a wide grin that flashed a set of flawless teeth. Being friends with Arabella should have given Max a serious inferiority complex, but somehow the two of them had largely avoided having any sort of rivalry or jealousy between them. It helped that Arabella's taste in men was wildly different from Max's. Her best friend behaved more like a protective older sister, always concerned for Max's best interests and attacking like an angry she-wolf whenever she saw her loved ones wronged. And then there were the actual bits of wolf-blood running through Arabella's veins. The things that made them different from the rest of humanity formed between them a bond of kinship that had proven unbreakable thus far.

Arabella was a lovely person, and Max considered herself lucky to have her as a friend. Still, it was impossible not to feel hideous whenever standing next to her. Having to wear sunglasses in order to hide an ugly snake-eye only accentuated that feeling this afternoon. Sinking deeper into Warrior Two, Max tried to clear her mind and stop stressing about imminent bills, lying to her boss, or the turbulence with Priest. She even ignored the curious glances from other students who no doubt wondered about the conspicuous eyewear. Despite her efforts, by the end of class, Max was no more relaxed than she had been when Priest stormed into her apartment.

Lying statue-still on her mat after everyone else had exited, Max kept her eyes closed, listening to one final pair of bare feet approach and stop next to her. She knew it was Arabella.

"Rough night?" her friend asked.

Max answered without opening her eyes. "It wasn't too bad. I got my guy."

Arabella sat next to Max on the floor, but a few seconds passed before she spoke again. "Are you talking about your bounty or Priest?"

Sighing, Max did her best to ignore the sudden constriction in her chest. It was pathetic that even the mention of his name had such an effect on her. "He called you, didn't he?"

"Nope. But you really should have showered."

"Oh." Max cringed inwardly. Sometimes she forgot about Arabella's enhanced sense of smell. "I guess there's no point in lying then." Rolling onto her side, Max pushed the sunglasses to the top of her head and faced the clear green eyes watching her intently. "He came over this morning," she admitted.

"And?"

"And nothing. We ended up fighting like always."

Arabella's expression was skeptical. "So, you two didn't have sex?"

"Well, no. Not really."

Arabella frowned. "What do you mean, not really? Either you had sex or you didn't. There's no such thing as kinda fucking."

"His penis did not get anywhere near my vagina."

"Okay so, it got near someplace else. That's still sex Max."

Max laughed. Arabella's dirty mind was one of many reasons why they were such good friends. "His penis got nowhere near there either."

Her best friend was undeterred. "What about your mouth? Did his penis get near there?"

"Ohmygod no."

"Don't say 'ohmygod no' to me like you're some kind of prude. You've done it a thousand times before."

Max rolled her eyes in exasperation. "Well, I have, but not this morning. Okay?"

"Uh huh." Arabella folded her arms. "What about *his* mouth?"

Max started to answer but then stopped, pursing her lips as a full-blown blush flooded her cheeks.

"I knew it!" Arabella basically shouted. "You are so not over him."

"I am too over him. I just had a moment of weakness."

Arabella snorted. "I'll say. What about Julien?"

A pang of regret shot through Max's belly. "I'm pretty sure we're over. And you can thank Priest for that. I let my guard down and the bastard seized the opening. Regardless, we probably would have ended up having sex if he hadn't insisted on starting a fight instead." Max shrugged in defeat. "I'm weak."

"Hold on a second." Arabella shook her head in disbelief. "Was Priest aware of it—that your resolve had crumbled to the point of having sex with him again?"

"Well, I was naked from the waist down, sweaty, and panting with lust. Oh, and his fingers were inside of me. So, yeah, I'd say he knew we were about to do some serious fornicating."

Arabella giggled. "And he stopped to pick a fight with you?" Her expression sobered. "It must have been for a really good reason."

Not liking the direction their conversation had abruptly taken, Max kept silent.

"Max?"

But Arabella wasn't going to let it go. Forcing a laugh, Max tried to keep her tone light. "Are you on his side now?"

"Ew. No." Arabella shook her head vigorously. "I'll always hate him for what he did to you, but even I can admit that Priest always has your best interests at heart. Even when he's being an idiot." She bit her lip, hesitating, and Max knew what would come next way before Arabella said it aloud. "You've been doing really well for some time now, Max. Don't go back to that dark place you were in."

"Not you too." Max groaned. "Priest *did* call you. Tell me exactly what he said."

"You went after a rabid kapre. Alone. What the hell were you thinking?"

"I called for help, Ari! Backup just didn't get there on time."

Arabella stretched her eyes in exasperation. "So, you just said, oh well, I'm going to take a rabid giant down by myself?"

"It was an open warrant. Other teams were coming, and I seriously needed the money."

"If things are that bad, just move back in with me and Jensen."

"I can't do that."

"And why the hell not?"

Max shrugged. "I don't know," she lied. The truth was too pathetic to admit. Truly, Max hoped that somehow her dad would notice her living on her own and taking care of things as a sure sign that she had fully recovered and was capable of looking after herself. She wanted him to stop sending goons like Priest to babysit her and otherwise treating her like a kid. Maybe if he saw her being a successful adult, he would back off, at least a little.

Arabella watched her steadily. She knew Max better than anyone else and probably wasn't fooled but didn't push. Though the worry never left her eyes, her frown softened. "You drive me crazy, you know that?"

"Yeah." Max stood and started rolling up her mat. "Sorry."

"Are you free to grab lunch, or is there a paranormal creature needing to be hunted down and jailed by Marshal Max?"

"My availability depends on whether you plan to continue badgering me about last night."

Arabella took Max by both shoulders. "As your best friend, I'm obligated to harass you for doing stupid shit."

"Whatever," Max said, but smiled in spite of herself. "I'll go for lunch, but we're getting tacos."

Arabella scrunched up her face. "What is your obsession with Mexican food?"

Max stared at her friend as if she had a third eye. "It's cheap, and it's delicious."

"Fine. Tacos it is. But we're not going to that nasty food truck that's always parked on Main Street."

"C'mon, they have the best tacos in town."

"That may be true, but the owner gives me the creeps."

"Arabella, you could rip his spleen from his body if he ever was crazy enough to try anything."

Her best friend folded her arms and stuck her nose in the air. "I probably could, but I don't really know where his spleen would be."

Max laughed. "Just Google that shit."

*

Sitting in a cramped, neon yellow booth opposite of Arabella, Max alternately glared at her friend and the menu. "I can't believe I let you drag me to this place." She flicked a stray piece of mystery meat off the table, left behind from the previous occupant. "Tacos and Coffee? Who thinks of that? And what kind of sick mind created these menu choices?"

"The kind of mind that wears distressed denim in thigh-hugging, skinny jeans and shirts that show off delicious biceps. Take those sunglasses off so you can appreciate this glorious view."

Without removing her shades, Max followed Arabella's hungry gaze and found the ballcap-wearing café manager, aka Arabella's next victim. He was an average-looking guy, but his body was definitely a ten on a scale of hotness. Max could practically smell the elevated testosterone lurking in his pores. With a normal girl, the guy probably reigned as alpha, but Arabella was no normal girl and was even less successful than Max in the dating ring. The carnage of her past relationships was just a long string of angry, bleeding hearts.

"So, we didn't come here for the food. This makes way more sense now."

"The tacos are good here," Arabella said without taking her eyes from the hunky manager, currently busy taking to-go orders from behind the front counter.

"Oh good, at least you've tasted the food. For a second, I was worried that you were only interested in ogling that poor guy until he was uncomfortable enough to call the cops."

Arabella was gorgeous, but her advances could be a little intimidating, to say the least. For starters, she had the kind of smile that was more like baring her teeth than an actual smile, effectively communicating cooperate or be killed. More predatory than flirtatious, her mannerisms clued in even the dimmest of men that they actually had little choice in whether to accept the good time the sway in her hips offered.

Across the room, the cafe manager was about to get a crash course in targeted heartbreak. Noticing Arabella's intense stare, his eyes widened even as his cheeks reddened. With an awkward smile, he quickly averted his gaze to the next customer.

Mission accomplished, Arabella returned her full attention to Max. "Oh no, I haven't eaten the tacos. But I have had the coffee. Don't order any. It's dreadful."

"Arabella, you're the worst. These tacos are five bucks a piece. I'm going to leave here hungry and unsatisfied."

"Don't stress over the price. I'm buying."

Max shook her head. "No way. You don't make that much more than me."

Giving a sly wink, Arabella took a sip of water. "Tips were great last night."

"Alrighty then. Our shitty lunch is on you."

"It can't be that bad." Arabella picked up the menu for the first time. After a few seconds, she made a repulsed expression. "Who the fuck would want to eat a pineapple hotdog taco?"

The waitress chose that moment to materialize to ask for their orders. "The Pine-Dog is one of our bestsellers."

They both gaped at the girl as if she had green skin and a third eye. "You've got to be kidding," Arabella said.

The waitress nodded cheerily. "Or if that doesn't interest you, try the Yellow-Mint Prime, our second bestseller. It's slow-cooked brisket marinated for twenty-fours in a cheddar-peppermint sauce."

Max winced. "I think I just threw up in my mouth."

Across the table, Arabella's face took on an ill note. She laid the menu down. "How about you just give us four plain tacos, please."

The waitress looked confused. "Plain?"

"Yes." Arabella pointed one perfectly manicured nail at the menu. "We want four of the Naked Ladies. Beef in a corn shell. Add lettuce, tomato, and cheese. *Plain* cheddar cheese," she added.

"Okay. Four Naked Ladies," the girl slowly repeated, sticking her tongue out in concentration as she jotted down the order. "Any coffee with that?"

"No," they answered in unison."

The waitress smiled. "Okay, I'll put this in and bring them out to you shortly."

Max leaned across the table when the girl was out of earshot. "Cancel our plans for tonight.

We're both going to the hospital once botulism sets in."

Arabella wrinkled her nose. "You might be right about that." Digging through her purse, she retrieved her cell phone. "Well, I can't let our imminent food poisoning be in vain. Be right back," she said, and left the table before Max could protest.

A few minutes later, Arabella returned, wearing a wolfish grin. She held up her cellphone. "Success."

"Let me guess," Max said. "You got the hunky manager's digits."

"We're going out tomorrow night."

"Wow. You don't waste time."

"Hey, no judging. A girl has needs, so I needs to get the ball rolling." Arabella laughed and flipped her silky hair. "Besides, Priest obviously satisfied you this morning, and I have shown an enormous amount of restraint in forgoing the lecture that you are due, slut."

"Touché."

"Speaking of Priest…" Arabella paused as the waitress returned with a tray of tacos overflowing with beef and cheddar, and set them on the table. "Am I still your date for the gala tonight?" she asked when the girl was gone.

"Yeah. You don't have to work, do you?" Max poked at the food, sniffing it before committing to a hesitant nibble. She was starving. At this point, cardboard likely would have tasted amazing.

"No, it's all boys at the club tonight. Should I wear a suit?"

"Don't be ridiculous." The taco actually wasn't bad. Throwing caution to the wind, Max took a larger bite. "Director Cranke only wants all his best agents there to shake hands and look pretty. He thinks the mayor needs to see who's protecting this city."

Arabella raised an eyebrow. "You're one of his best agents?"

"Don't be an asshole."

Arabella laughed. "I'm sorry, Max. You don't exactly have the best track record."

"Uh huh." Max wasn't going to take the bait. "So, what does tonight's gala have to do with Priest?"

"He might have mentioned that he's handling security there."

Inhaling when she should have swallowed, Max sucked a blob of food down prematurely, sending her lungs into a spasmodic fit of coughing. Eyes watering, she gulped water and cleared her throat until the obstruction passed and she could breathe normally again. All the while, Arabella continued to eat, smirking between mouthfuls.

"Please say you're just screwing with me," Max croaked.

Arabella laughed. "Yeah, and clearly it was a terrible joke. I almost feel bad about it."

"Tell me, why are we friends again?"

"Because you're a glutton for punishment."

Max rolled her eyes. "Obviously."

Finishing the last bit of food in her basket, Arabella crumbled the wax paper into a ball and chucked it onto the tray. "Come over later, and I'll do your makeup."

"I can do my own makeup."

"For everyday wear, you do okay, but tonight is special. We're going to be in sparkly gowns."

"I'm not wearing sparkles."

Arabella let out a frustrated sigh. "Ohmygod just come over later."

"Alright. Alright, I will. I just need to go home and get some sleep first."

"I won't argue with that." Arabella stood up. "I'm going to go take care of the bill. See you later."

"Wait. Where are you rushing off to?" Max asked, expecting a scandalous answer. It was Arabella after all.

"Four nights ago, I promised Jensen that I'd wash the dishes. If he wakes up and sees the kitchen is still trashed, he might be too mad to switch shifts with me tomorrow. And I really need to get laid."

Max shook her head. "You are a fascinating creature."

"I know," Arabella agreed, and blew Max a quick kiss. "Ciao, Bella."

*

A few hours later, Max woke up to the insistent wail of an alarm she'd set after arriving back at her apartment. Foggy with sleep, she reached over and silenced her cellphone. Ten more minutes wouldn't hurt anything. Looping through the cycle three more times, Max eventually rolled off the sofa and stumbled into the bathroom.

Ugh, she couldn't help thinking as she glanced at her haggard-looking reflection in the mirror. She looked like hell. It would take either a modern-day miracle or a two-inch spackling of makeup to make her beautiful tonight. Damn. Sleep should have made things better, not worse.

After splashing cold water on her face, Max reached for a fresh pair of contact lenses to mask the snake eye and darken her golden irises. At least the nap had made it possible to wear contacts again. Her face was about six inches from the mirror with one finger poised to insert a lens when Priest materialized in the doorway. Max jerked in surprise, swearing as the contact slipped from her finger and fluttered to the floor.

Naked except for the towel wrapped about his waist, Priest's muscular and tattooed torso glistened with droplets from a recent shower. He was smiling one of his rare smiles that made his blue eyes light up from within. Max hadn't seen him smile like that in a very long time…since before their breakup.

"What the hell are you doing in here?"

Unfazed by the anger in her tone, Priest strode toward her with the grace of a jungle cat, bicep rippling as he curled one arm to run a hand through his damp, spiked hair. A silver chain dangled from his neck—one Max never remembered seeing—securing a pair of worn dog tags. Max squinted. Those weren't familiar either. But something else was far more concerning—Priest's unusual silence. After breaking into her apartment twice in one day, he should have been completely full of himself. Gloating about his prowess, not staring at her with creepy admiration.

"Priest?" she said uncertainly. Fighting the urge to back away, she ignored her screaming instincts.

Then he reached her, and the security Max always felt in his presence, enveloped her like a warm blanket. The smile had disappeared, replaced by a smoldering gaze that singed every part it touched. Resting one hand against her cheek, Priest tilted his head as if he might kiss her, overwhelming Max with the soft cinnamon-tinged musk of his natural scent floating beneath her favorite rainforest body wash. She closed her eyes to shut out at least one assault on her senses, cutting off part of the ache now stirring in her scarred heart.

"Maybe I should just go through your heart," he whispered.

"What?"

Priest thrust his hips forward, and Max got the idea. She didn't need x-ray vision to know what was going on beneath that towel, feeling the thick bulge grow longer and harder until it dug firmly into her belly, begging to be inside of her. Moisture slickened her panties as Max thought of exactly how amazing that would feel, and then Priest moved his hips again, slowly grinding against her, teasing her with his massive erection, coaxing a soft sigh from her lips. Hormones and emotion had overridden whatever caution instinct urged. The attraction was too strong, especially when his beautifully tattooed and muscled torso was slick with water, and his hard thighs and even harder cock were pressed against her body.

Max trembled. Her fingers twitched at her sides, still torn between pulling away and pulling him to the floor for a marathon session of ~~lovemaking~~ incredible sex.

"Damn you, Priest," she whispered.

"Max don't."

At the sudden urgency in his voice, her eyes flew wide open, and what she saw nearly made her scream. Priest was bleeding…badly. Blood gushed from his neck and beneath his ribs where a huge wound split apart the dark inked dragon that curled around his torso. The towel about his waist was soaked with blood. More of it dripped to the tiled floor and pooled into the grout. Even more frightening was the fear in Priest's eyes. Max had never seen him afraid, and to witness it now sent a chill through her entire existence.

Though realizing the entire moment had to somehow be all in her head, she reached for him anyway because if she could feel him, then—real or not—Priest needed her and maybe she could help him. It was flawed, silly logic, but that was the effect Priest had on her.

As soon as her fingers touched him, blood poured over Max's hand, defying gravity to travel upward until her entire arm was engulfed in red. Everywhere the ghastly liquid touched, burned her skin like the sting of one hundred fire ants, but Max refused to let go. The terror in Priest's expression faded as his eyes changed from sapphire to white and then to silver.

She gasped as the pain in her arm radiated into her neck and skull, threatening to tear her apart from the inside. Lungs crushed by an unseen force, Max wanted to scream, but couldn't. There was no air. Squeezing her eyes shut against the agony, she held onto Priest and begged the pain to stop.

Falling forward, she caught herself just short of collapse, taking in a huge breath of air as her lungs finally did their fucking job and expanded. Max coughed violently, choking on air as if her body had forgotten how to breathe. At least the pain was gone. So was the blood…and so was Priest.

Dazed, Max stumbled out of the bathroom and searched the apartment to confirm that she was in fact alone. Every room was empty, her labored breaths the only sound.

Anxiously dragging both hands through her tangled hair, Max bit back a sob. "What the hell?"

She hurried back to the bathroom, flung open the cabinet above the sink, and snatched a half-empty pill bottle from the top shelf. Taking several deep breaths, Max aimed a dazed stare at the bottle and went into the living room. After turning in a slow circle, she sank to the couch and sat very still, seriously needing a moment to compose herself as she searched her brain and tried to decipher what had just happened. Maybe Arabella, Kevin, and Priest had all been right to be so concerned.

Inside the bottle, the pills rattled in her trembling hand. This wasn't her first hallucination, but this one felt different from the rest. Max didn't need pills. Being stressed and sleep deprived had caused this. She didn't always react to things like normal humans, so maybe this was simply her mind's way of dealing with an overload. Only Max didn't feel overloaded. She felt as if she had been handling things pretty well for a long stretch now.

"Screw it," she muttered and stood up, abruptly realizing what—no who—the problem was. Priest. He had barged into her apartment this morning, destroyed her latest relationship, and then nearly charmed his way back into her vagina. That was enough to trigger a minor setback in anyone with her history.

Tossing the pills back into the cabinet, she slammed it shut, washed her face for a second time. "You're okay," she whispered while staring into the mirror. Calm again, Max squared her shoulders and lowered herself to the floor. She needed to find the contact she'd dropped earlier. Two minutes later, both lenses were in and Max looked human again.

From the bedroom closet, she grabbed a gown that was carefully wrapped in clear plastic. From beneath the bed, she retrieved a pair of strappy heels and a thigh holster for a small pistol. Last but not least, she made sure to get the wig reserved for only the most special occasions. It was beautiful—made from long, silky, jet black hair. When Max wore it, she turned heads for all the right reasons.

Conducting a quick once-over of the apartment, Max was certain she had the necessary building blocks for an appearance that wouldn't make her look like an ugly step-sister in comparison to her genetically blessed best friend. She eventually left the apartment feeling confident. Arabella was practically Picasso when it came to makeup. So, if anyone could camouflage puffy eyes, dry skin, and chapped lips, Arabella was her best bet.

Halfway to the third-floor landing, Max swore and turned back. She had forgotten the car keys. Even if she didn't have so many things to carry with her, walking wasn't a viable way to travel to the duplex that Arabella shared with a roommate. The duplex was twenty minutes away by car, located across the bridge in a tiny borough that showcased more houses than residents. Max had liked the solitude of living there, but the distance from work had been a significant inconvenience. Arabella and Jensen didn't seem to mind though. The two of them both worked in the city, commuting by subway several nights a week to take the stage at Gents & Belles. The apartment where Max now lived was more centrally located in the territory she covered. It meant faster response times, and that translated to more captures and money in Max's bank account.

She had barely knocked twice when Arabella opened the door. Looking Max up and down, Arabella shook her head. "You're late."

"Sorry, I overslept." Max double-checked her watch. "By like five minutes." She couldn't tell Arabella about what had happened in her apartment. If her friend was worried before, hearing about a vivid hallucination would freak her out beyond measure.

"Five minutes could mean life or death in your line of work."

"We're putting on makeup and dresses for a charity ball. Your argument does not apply here."

Arabella folded her arms. "Now that's a poor attitude to have. Tonight, your face is representing all forty-nine marshals of the southern districts."

Max blinked. Arguing was futile. "Are you going to let me in?"

"If you promise to have a better attitude."

"Seriously?"

Raising one eyebrow, Arabella lifted her chin a touch higher.

Max took a deep breath. Sometimes, Arabella enjoyed pushing her buttons for pure amusement. Deep down, Max sometimes wondered if their friendship was actually penance for past sins in another life. "I will have a better attitude," she humbly conceded. "I am at your mercy."

Arabella smiled. "Now that's more like it." Swinging the door wide, she stepped to the side and made a little curtsey. "Come in, my princess. Magic awaits you."

"You're ridiculous."

"But you love me anyway." Smiling sweetly, Arabella shoved a bottle of water into Max's hands. "Drink this. All of it. Your pores are terrible."

Max sighed. "Yes ma'am."

Five

Vanity had never been one of Max's vices, but tonight, she really could not stop looking at herself. Max could not believe that she was the beauty who stared back in her own reflection. Arabella deserved a bottle of twelve-year bourbon and a steak dinner for this fabulous transformation. Casting aside the black dress Max originally brought over, Arabella had put Max in one of her own barely worn gowns. Glittery, clingy, and golden, the dress had several cutouts at the sides and back. Arabella had even convinced Max to ditch the wig and wear her natural hair, pulled back into a fancy up-do made possible by the grace of nearly an entire jar of hair gel and Arabella's unrelenting tenacity.

Even standing arm in arm with Arabella— who was as beautiful as ever in the simple black dress from Max's closet that clung to every curve while showcasing some serious cleavage— people still noticed Max. Envy, adoration, lust— name the look and Max got it from men and women alike. Even the mayor's much younger wife had seemed awestruck—graciously complimenting Max's appearance during an earlier meet and greet.

"I told you to trust me," Arabella said, beaming proudly. "You're gorgeous."

Max patted her friend's hand gratefully. "You know how much I hate crowds, but tonight, I'm okay."

"Tonight, the crowd loves you, Bella."

Blushing with embarrassment, Max smiled. "Thank you."

"You're welcome. Now stand tall and pretend to be a good agent because here comes your boss."

Freezing a pleasant smile in place, Max spoke through her teeth in an annoyed whisper, "I am a good agent."

By way of reply, Arabella squeezed Max's hand, keeping in whatever sassy retort she had in store. Max would probably hear it later.

Director Cranke approached, looking rather dashing in a nicely tailored tuxedo. Despite rumors claiming he hated the political side of his job, he certainly did an excellent job of blending in. Always calm and always in control, no one knew what the director was thinking unless he told them.

"I almost didn't recognize you, marshal." His gaze roamed up and down the length of Max's body as he shook his head in amazement. "You're stunning."

"Wow. Aren't you charming," Arabella said flatly.

Director Cranke shifted his attention to Arabella as if noticing her for the first time. If he was at all affected by her knockout figure and dazzling beauty, he certainly didn't show it. "That did sound rather rude of me. I apologize, marshal. Usually, I'm so careful with my words. I guess your loveliness, along with the complimentary spirits have thrown me off my game."

"Thank you, Director, but I took no offense. My friend, Arabella, gets a little overprotective sometimes."

The director's lips pulled into a thin, humorless smile that never quite reached his eyes. "I never took you as the sort to require protection, marshal."

"I'm not," Max replied promptly. *Though my father would disagree.*

"Very well. Thanks for being here tonight. Play your cards right, and you'll have a very bright future, young lady." Moving a step back, Director Cranke inclined his head in a slight bow. "Ladies," he said, and then mingled into the crowd once more.

"So, that's Cranky Kevin, huh?"

"Yeah."

"And he's your boss?" Arabella's eyes followed him across the room.

"Um, yeah."

"He's cute."

"Really? I mean, I guess so. He does look great in that tux." Max wasn't sure she liked the twinkle in Arabella's eyes. "C'mon, Ari. You can't seduce my boss."

"Why not? Is he married?"

Max blinked. She honestly didn't know the answer to that. "Because he's my boss, that's why. Things could get ugly…and awkward."

"You're already awkward."

"Gee. Thanks." Max tucked an errant golden tendril behind her ear, saying a silent prayer that the half of a dozen hair products responsible for keeping her from being mistaken for an African lion somehow lasted through the night. "I'm going to get a drink and then some air. You want to come with, or are you okay here?"

"I'll take you up on the drink, but there's way too much eye candy going on out here for me to hide away with you. Stay and mingle, Max. It'll be good for your self-esteem."

"My self-esteem is fine, Ari," Max argued as they moved toward the stairway. "I'm just feeling slightly claustrophobic and a little too sober for the occasion."

"Suit yourself. If I get lost, don't wait up," Arabella said with an exaggerated a wink.

Max laughed. "Trust me. I know better."

Despite the surprising throng of people crowding the upstairs bar, she and Arabella were able to order drinks almost immediately, thanks to her friend's shameless flirting. Capturing a pair of vodka martinis from the baby-faced bartender, Arabella handed one to Max and raised her glass in a toast. "Here's to staying positive and testing negative."

Tapping their drinks together, they each took a generous swig of martini, kissed each other on the cheek, and parted ways. Arabella went prowling for a good time, and Max climbed two flights of stairs to leave the crowd behind, wandering until she found an exit leading to the roof that wouldn't trigger an alarm once opened. Immensely relieved to breathe the crisp night air and stand beneath a brilliant crescent moon, she leaned against the terrace railing and quietly reflected on the past twenty-four hours.

She really was lucky to be alive. Walking out of the forest after a fierce battle with a maddened giant who possessed an undocumented, game-changing ability was an incredible feat, but now Max was left with a debt to Kalista Darkesong that she wasn't sure she could ever repay.

What hadn't survived was her relationship with Julien. He wasn't taking any of her calls, and she had yet to hear from him since this morning when he'd fled in terror from her apartment. Max wasn't holding her breath. Few people stuck around after seeing the real Maxima Masters.

It was a bitter thought. She drained the rest of the vodka martini to wash it down.

Really, Max didn't know whether to hate Priest or thank him. She'd never had much luck in the romance department. Her love life was all about picking the wrong guy or finding the right guy at the wrong time. One after the other, they were always too controlling or too weak, too boring or too crazy. But on the day Max's path had crossed with Priest's, that all changed. From the first moment they met, he had burrowed under her skin. Admittedly, it had taken a little longer for her to get under his. Sometimes it felt as if Max had known Priest from another lifetime. Even more ridiculous was believing her soul had known the truth before she did—but even now, she still couldn't admit it.

"I thought all law enforcement were required to be armed tonight."

Max simultaneously bristled and melted at the sound of his voice. *So, Arabella wasn't kidding after all.* "How long have you been watching me?" she asked without turning around.

Priest answered without hesitation. "Since the day I met you," he said softly.

She smiled despite herself. At least he couldn't see it. *Words. Words. Words.* "Oh, you deserve applause for that one. Flattery and dodging my question at the same time." She uttered a short laugh. "So, what made you lower yourself to this level? I didn't think security was your thing."

"A threat was identified." His deep, silky tone drew nearer, but Max couldn't discern the sound of his footsteps. Priest was sneaky like that. "And the governor's regular detail isn't trained to handle it."

She shrugged her slender shoulders, steeling her body against a sudden and forceful gust of wind. "Politicians get threatened all the time. Comes with the territory."

"Well, this threat curiously coincides with a recent uptick in activity from the rifts. Lab geeks responsible for monitoring the situation discovered a huge energy spike several weeks back. It's a sure indication that something really powerful crossed over." Still low and smooth, his voice sharpened into focus as he closed in on her vulnerable position. "No creature that explains the surge has been spotted, but reports of missing persons have increased."

"Yeah," Max said slowly. "Missing persons aren't really your thing either, so I'm thinking that one or more of these missing persons are of significant importance."

"That's classified."

She pursed her lips. "Of course," she said and finally moved to face him. He had stopped a few feet away—every gorgeous and imposing inch of him standing just outside of the shadows. Tonight, instead of the all-black militant style of dress grunts like him preferred, Priest actually wore a suit. Still in all black from head to toe, the only thing of color was the shiny, blue bow tie around his neck. Illuminated by a swath of moonlight, Priest really could have been one of the enchanting, perilous creatures he so often hunted.

A long and tense silence hung between them while his savage eyes drilled into Max, peeling back every layer of who she was…starting with her clothes. It would have been nice to match that intensity, to make him feel the pressure for a change, but doing so would have meant having to admit to Priest—at least with her eyes—that she desperately wanted to fuck him again.

"That's a great dress," he said, breaking the silence and moving closer. "I'd love to see how you're concealing a weapon underneath there."

"Would you also love a black eye?" She placed a hand on his chest, but Priest was immovable. So, Max slid backward, moving against the rail to put some distance between them. Up close, she was glad to see no evidence of the shallow scratches she'd left on his face eleven hours ago. "That's far enough."

Priest grinned. His smile was as dangerous as ever. "I can take whatever punishment you want to give me, Maxima. You know I like it rough."

Max gulped. Wondering why it was so damned hard to say no to him, she clenched the martini glass tighter, as if it could be a totem against his magic. "What's gotten into you all of a sudden? I barely hear from you for months and now I've had to practically peel you off of me twice in the same day."

As she spoke, the charm and self-assurance faltered, allowing Max a glimpse of raw emotion Priest rarely let through. A split second later, the transparency was gone, but his gaze remained earnest. "When you didn't report in this morning," he said, covering her hand with his, "I didn't know what to think. And until I knew you were safe, my entire world stopped."

"Oh," was all she managed.

Slipping one arm around her waist, Priest pulled her body flush to his. Max didn't resist. This unprecedented bout of honesty had gotten to her. Trying to recover her senses, she enjoyed the feel of his body pressed against her. Even after everything, Priest still felt like home. She was safe with him…only that wasn't true. His betrayal had proven that.

"I don't ever want to feel that again," he said gruffly, crashing through her thoughts. "And if I can't reach that stubborn head of yours through reason, then maybe I should just go through your body." His other hand moved to her chest, resting over her traitorous heart, currently pounding louder than the hooves of a galloping herd. "Through your heart," he whispered and gently cupped her breast.

Startled at his words, Max jerked away, but the hand on her back tightened, holding her in place. "What did you just say?" she croaked hoarsely, remembering that only hours before, she had hallucinated Priest saying the exact same thing.

Instead of answering, Priest lowered his mouth to her skin, following the neckline of her dress with a series of kisses that melted her core and resolve with equal efficiency. By the time he had finished, lifting his head to meet her eyes, Max was quivering with desire. His touch had set her skin afire, awakening a familiar and irresistible hunger. Now his burning gaze held her captive. Wanting to look away and save herself, Max was powerless to do so. She realized again, what she had many times before.

This man will be my undoing.

Max gritted her teeth. She couldn't do this. Priest was toxic. This morning she had been weak and drank from the poisoned well. This afternoon, she'd almost needed pills to cope. There was only one conclusion—being with Priest threatened her recovery.

"Priest," she began weakly, but the regret on her face must have said it all.

"Don't." He shook his head, closing his eyes with a pained expression. "I know what you're going to say, but don't. I can't ever change what I did to you." He stopped as his voice became thick and uneven. "But I'll forever regret it. I'll never put orders before you again, Max. I swear it."

Tears in her eyes, Max couldn't meet that earnest gaze any longer. She wanted to believe him. She wanted to let go and give into what her every cell desired, but she couldn't. Though it hadn't been Priest wearing the mask and white coats, jamming needles into her body and forcing her to undergo hours upon hours of grueling tests, he had been the one who delivered her to those madmen. And simply because her father had told him to.

"I can't, Priest. I'm sorry."

He stroked her cheek, wiping away the tears that fell there. "They say every day is supposed to be easier. But it isn't. I'm in hell without you, Maxima."

On the inside, Max was crying hysterically. "You're going to be alright," she promised, flabbergasted by the control in her voice. Maybe she did have some sense of self-preservation after all.

Priest let go of her then, and the frigid air rushed in, chilling Max's body through the gown's thin material. Funny how she hadn't noticed the cold before. "No," he said. "I don't think I will."

His voice had never sounded so fraught with loss, and Max wanted to hold him, to deliver him from the guilt that tortured his soul. Giving into that urge, she reached for him, but it was too late. Priest was already gone.

*

Groaning, Max face-planted into the pillow. Mentally exhausted, the only thing she wanted was sleep but knew it wouldn't come for a long time, if at all. Her thoughts were pure turmoil. After Priest disappeared from the rooftop, Max had lacked the will to rejoin the party. So she'd climbed down the fire escape and walked three blocks before hailing a cab, nervous during the entire wait that her clandestine exit would be foiled by a well-meaning best friend. By the time she got back to her apartment and languished beneath a hot shower, the storm of emotions that threatened to wreck her sanity had mostly abated. Now Max was simply drained. She didn't want to think about Priest anymore. Or her father. Or her job. Or her kinda screwed up life. Max just wanted to sleep, but like everything else she wanted, that too evaded her.

Abandoning the losing struggle, she switched on the bedside lamp and decided to work on Friday night's kapre report. Since being completely truthful meant getting good people in trouble, Max resigned to committing a few lies of omission. She couldn't mention Kalista Darkesong or the fact that she had received backup at all for the takedown. Inventing some mysterious savior would only arouse more questions, followed by suspicion and/or discovery when she couldn't properly answer them.

Max typed, leaving out major details regarding the moments in battle with Nihilson, but an explanation was needed as to why she was only able to salvage the tree giant's teeth as proof of kill. After some musing, all attempts at live capture only resulted in failure and she nearly lost her life in the process. As a last result, she had set a trap for the giant, doused him with a special accelerant, and then regrettably set him on fire, thereby terminating the diseased creature.

Lifting her hands from the keyboard, Max reviewed the report. Thus far, it was a slightly incredible, but believable, story. She had taken great care to emphasize the giant's previously undocumented ability to camouflage itself as a major deciding factor of the kapre's ultimate fate. Hopefully, her superiors would see that she was left little choice in the matter. If Nihilson hadn't been put down in such a manner, USPMS would have lost their second agent this year.

Rubbing her eyes, Max yawned. At least she was sleepy now. It was one of paperwork's most reliable side effects. Leaning against the headboard, she started to nod off but then her cellphone vibrated across the nightstand, startling her awake. Max frowned. *This had better be seriously important.*

Checking the display, she saw that a blanket 911 alert had been sent to every agent, requesting their immediate presence at the agency. Max couldn't recall ever being summoned from her home in the middle of the night to attend a meeting. Something huge had happened. Or something awful.

Fighting the growing sense of dread that steadily built within her cells, she hurriedly dressed in black jeans and a long-sleeved, cotton shirt of the same color. A mid-weight jacket bearing the insignia of the Paranormal Marshal Services completed the ensemble. Then Max ran a hairbrush through her thick mane, pulling it back into a ponytail before tying the frizzy tresses into a low knot. Choosing a short black wig styled in an angled bob, she covered her natural locks and secured the wig firmly in place with over half a dozen bobby pins. Brown contacts to camouflage the weirdly shaped pupil and darken her golden-colored eyes were the final piece of the charade. After years of practice, the routine took less than ten minutes.

Securing the Shrike tomahawk between her shoulders and holstering the revolver at her hip, Max left her apartment, armed and ready for whatever trouble awaited. She had a feeling she might be hunting tonight.

*

When Max arrived at USPMS, the thirteenth-floor lobby was crawling with agents. Most were dressed in all black and stood shoulder to shoulder—or in some cases, shoulder to head. Many of the marshals boasted altered genetics, byproducts of experiments conducted during tours of military service. Their abilities were enhanced, granting them incredible speed and the strength of three men, making them extremely capable fighters. And there were even those among the marshals who had never been human.

Max rapidly did a headcount of the marshals present in attendance. Only forty-three of the forty-nine were present. At least she wasn't last.

The second thing Max noticed—which should have probably been the first—was that the double steel doors, usually sealed by biometric security measures to bar access to restricted areas, stood wide open. That was odd. And quite alarming.

Easing her way deeper into the throng of marshals, Max took a position between Alyn and Oz. Each well over six feet tall, Alyn and Oz were two excellent examples of agents who had never been human. Deadly in their own right, moonlight caused a frightening transformation within their Kindred blood, changing them into nightmarish, wolf-troll creatures. Kindred were one of the few inhuman species indigenous to earth, possessing both abilities and savagery that served them and their government well. They were good guys and even better marshals. For every bounty that Max successfully recovered, Alyn and Oz apprehended or eliminated three. But, Max argued, if their success rate were divvied up between them, those guys only averaged 1.5 captures apiece.

On a personal level, Max didn't know a whole lot about them. Only that they were cousins and former members of a disbanded pack…or something like that. Both had distractingly muscular biceps, an affinity for knives, and a peculiar wildness about them. Supposedly, that uniquely feral energy was innate to their species.

Max nudged Oz in the side. "What's going on," she whispered.

Oz's forest green eyes sharpened as they looked down at her. "You don't smell it?"

"No." Max frowned slightly. She was strong and fast, but would never have a Kindred sense of smell. But Oz already knew that. "If you guys are Bloodhounds, then I'm a Chihuahua. What do you smell?"

"Death," Alyn answered.

Shit. Max had been right. Something awful had happened.

"Who?"

"Dunno yet." Oz's mouth settled into a grim line. "But how odd that with all this commotion, our fine director is nowhere in sight."

Sickened to the core, Max realized Oz was right. She licked her lips, uneasily considering the possible scenarios. Maybe Director Cranke was busy elsewhere dealing with this mess. A murder inside of a high-profile, government building had to be a security as well as a political nightmare. Since Max had left the gala early, it was also probable that Director Cranke was still detained there, schmoozing increased funding from the mayor. The likelihood of her conjectures plummeted when a pair of figures stepped through the open doorway. Director Cranke wasn't at the gala or off somewhere managing blowback.

Having ditched all formal attire, Priest was now dressed in tactical pants and combat boots with assorted weapons fastened to his waist and thighs. Beneath an armor-plated vest, the fitted shirt he wore had both sleeves rolled up, showcasing two abundantly tattooed forearms. But in stark contrast to the militant uniform, his platinum-colored hair remained slickly styled from the gala. Blue eyes glittering in the ultraviolent light, Priest surveyed the crowd with a stare harder than the steel doors behind him. Max found herself wondering how it was possible for a guy to be so gorgeous and dangerous at the same time.

Few in the room knew Priest. As agents of USPMS, all marshals were ultimately subject to the control of the Unified Combatant Command—a coalition between the United States military and the securities division of a private civilian corporation called Global Cures. Their combined mission was to keep the world safe from paranormal threats. Priest's assignment within the UCC was very different from Max's. He belonged to a secret division of independent operators, elite strike forces tasked to eliminate the biggest and most dangerous threats. His squad left minimal collateral and no witnesses. They were known as ghosts within the UCC.

Examining the throng of co-workers, Max could easily differentiate between the marshals who knew Priest and those who didn't. Awe and suspicion lined the faces of the handful who did, while the rest had errantly assumed Priest was just some pretty boy playing dress up, only pretending to be a soldier. A blend of contempt and impatience was evident by their body language, or barely concealed in their expressions.

Max didn't recognize the woman who stood next to Priest. On the shorter side, with chocolate-colored skin and dark, curly hair, the woman spoke in a loud, commanding voice that belied her petite stature. "I am Captain Abbot Knox, and I will be serving as the interim director of this agency until further notice." She paused. "Director Cranke is dead."

Letting that statement hang on a wave of murmurs that immediately erupted, Cpt. Knox waited for their shocked voices to fall silent. Like everyone else, Max was having a difficult time getting her brain to accept what was happening. She had just spoken to the director only hours before. And now he was dead?

"This level has been sealed," Cpt. Knox continued. "And it will remain so until each of you have been interviewed by First Sergeant Preesti and his team. First Sergeant Preesti is leading the investigation into Director Cranke's murder. Give him your full cooperation. Once all of you have been cleared, assignments will be issued at his discretion. Together we will find the piece of filth that did this."

Murder?

Max jerked in surprise when Oz squeezed her arm. "He was killed here, but he put up a fight," the tall Kindred whispered. "Prepare yourself."

She frowned. "Did your nose also tell you who killed him?"

Cpt. Knox started speaking again. "If your last name begins with a letter between A and F, step forward please."

Oz's cool fingers tightened around Max's arm once more. "Just be ready, Masters." Then he and Alyn obeyed the new interim director's first order by moving to the front of the room.

Absently rubbing her arm, Max noticed Priest watching her. As his fierce gaze locked onto hers, Max's heart missed three successive beats.

His eyes never leaving her, he spoke above the crowd without raising his voice. "Marshal Masters, report with group one."

Shit.

Too many heads turned in Max's direction. They were likely only curious about the significance of her being singled out for the ~~interrogations~~ interviews, but to Max, the moment felt like one from grade school when she was the golden-haired, snake-eyed freak in the corner, being gawked at by all the normal kids.

As Max made her way to the open corridor where a huddle of other marshals waited to be escorted, she saw Cute Kevin standing at the edge of the crowd, bearing no resemblance to the handsome charmer that he was. His skin was ashen. A thin sheen of sweat had broken out all over his face, and two very bloodshot eyes completed the ghastly look. Kevin was either about to puke or pass out.

Delaying Priest's order, she went to her friend and grasped his hand. "Kevin?" she said gently. At first, he continued to stare straight ahead, but then slowly, his eyes found her face. Recognition took a few seconds longer.

"Oh god, Max," he choked. Those three words were fraught with terror and something else Max could not readily place. He was barely holding it together.

Please don't fall apart. Please don't fall apart. She gave his hand another firm squeeze "Kevin, it's going to be okay," she assured him.

"Masters," Priest urged in a tone hinting at impatience.

Ignoring him, Max kept her attention exactly where it was needed. "Just take deep breaths. I'll come back and we can talk about it. Okay?"

Swallowing hard, Kevin nodded. Then Max pulled away and followed Priest into the sequestered hallway that stretched out before her like a dimly lit and carpeted mile, wondering why her pulse was suddenly pounding so fast. She had a terrible feeling about all of this.

Stalling his pace slightly until she caught up, Priest passed a worried glance over her. "Are you okay?"

Max nodded. "I'm dealing."

Stopping just outside a pair of oak doors leading to conference room two, Priest rubbed the nape of his neck. "It's not pretty in there. Something chewed him up bad." He started to say more, but fell silent as a scowl crossed his features. A second later, a tall figure emerged from the shadows just beyond them. It was Oz. His partner was nowhere in sight.

"I have already warned her," he said softly, while slowly stalking toward them with an odd, raptorial grace.

Priest's frowned deepened. A hard edge crept into his voice as he addressed the Kindred. "You should be inside, Dezmoon. Where is your escort?"

"Escort?" Oz tilted his head in puzzlement. "Am I a suspect now, Sergeant?"

In a blur of motion, Priest moved to close the remaining distance between him and the Kindred. Oz was a big guy, but so was Priest. They stood eye to eye, each side bristling with tamed aggression. Max recognized a cock fight when she saw one. She just didn't understand what this one was about.

"That's First Sergeant," he said quietly. "And everyone is a suspect until I deem otherwise."

"Is Masters a suspect as well?"

Priest's right eye twitched almost imperceptibly. It was only with Max that he openly expressed emotion, whether it be anger, joy, or sadness. Professionally, Priest was the textbook image of calm and control. By the time he lost his temper publicly, the subject of his ire was already dead.

When he spoke again, his voice held an eerie calm. "Report to the area you were assigned to, and do not leave your escort again."

Oz opened his mouth, but then appeared to think better of it. Pulling himself to full attention, he turned on heel and strode down the hallway toward the east section.

Max exhaled a tense breath she hadn't realized she was holding. "What was that about?"

"The hell if I know. Is he a friend of yours?"

"I trust him."

Priest flashed a humorless smile. "That's not what I asked."

"No," Max said, folding her arms. "Oz and I are not friends. But he wears the same badge I do. That means if I need him, he has my back."

"He doesn't seem to like me very much."

"That's because you're an asshole, Priest. No one likes you."

"You like me."

Max pursed her lips. Even at a serious time like this, he couldn't resist an opening to get under her skin. But she wasn't in the mood to entertain him.

"That's okay." Priest's smile was genuine now. "You don't have to admit it." He edged closer, invading her space with six feet and five imposing inches of hardened muscle and brooding danger. "You know what else I know?"

Max knew she should move away from him, but couldn't bring herself to do it because he was gravity. Using sarcasm, she tried to mask how much he affected her. "Please tell me, Harrison. The suspense is killing me."

"A blind guy could see that Dezmoon worships the ground you walk on."

"On a night like this, you choose to be jealous."

"Ah. So, you're not denying it."

"No, because you're being ridiculous. Why did you call me here ahead of so many others, Priest? Am I a suspect?"

"Everyone is at this point. So, officially yes." He slid one palm against her cheek, gently cupping her face. "But not to me. Never to me, Max."

Searching his face, she saw nothing except sincerity and wanted to believe she could trust him. *Maybe you can.* Max closed her eyes.

"Stop running from me."

"If you would stop chasing me, I wouldn't have to."

"I'm not gonna stop, Max."

"Priest."

"I know. You can't. But I'm not gonna stop." Releasing her, he stepped back. "We've got a job to do."

"Right." Max smoothed her hair down and tried to collect her wits. "My boss was murdered tonight. Let's worry about that."

Priest held the door open. "After you."

It didn't take long to discern why the building was on lockdown and everyone was being treated so aggressively. The conference room was a mess. Oz had been right. Director Cranke had put up a fight. But it hadn't been enough.

Even before Max saw the body, she saw the blood. So much blood. The walls, floor, and even the ceiling were all smeared in red. Chunks of fleshy matter were scattered about, stuck to chairs, and settling deep into the carpet's fibers. Max was super mindful of where she placed each step. The last thing she wanted to do was inadvertently take home any of Cranky Kevin's mushy bits.

Well, I guess he isn't Cranky Kevin anymore. Now he's Dead Kevin.

At least the shoes she wore were actually suited for the job. If a false step were taken, a little blood wouldn't hurt her government issued boots.

"Watch out," Priest said, grabbing her elbow.

Max looked down. Good save. She was being careful, but obviously not careful enough. Her foot was poised to squish a detached eyeball.

"Thanks," Max whispered.

"Anytime." Priest released her.

Max was grateful. The less he touched her, the better. It was certainly easier to think more clearly. "You can definitely eliminate anything or anyone vampiric from your list. A creature like that wouldn't have let all this go to waste."

Priest nodded. "I agree."

"Show me the rest of him."

"This way."

Through the conference room, he led her into another hallway. There was more blood here, a broad streaking smudge of it that lasted for several yards, as if a body had been dragged for some distance. Maneuvering around the large carpet stains, Priest opened the door to a private office. It wasn't the director's, but it was large, situated in a corner, and had a great view. It had to belong to someone important…someone who wasn't going to be very happy on Monday morning.

Max peered at Kevin Cranke's remains and barely recognized them as human. She noticed blood coated shreds of material that could have been pieces of the tux he'd worn to tonight's gala, but his clothing, like his body, was in shambles.

Glistening shards of bone and cartilage protruded from the wreckage of what was once a chest cavity. Hunks of muscle, flaps of skin, and unidentifiable morsels were haphazardly strewn about. Joints were disarticulated. Hands and feet dismembered. Internal organs entirely or partially missing as if an animal had started to feed but was interrupted.

And the stench...

Max considered Priest. With his much more pronounced sense of smell, it was incredible that he was able to tolerate being in the room with this bloodied pile of meat, much less show absolutely no sign of being bothered. Then again, Priest had probably seen a lot worse in his line of work.

"Where the fuck is his head?" she asked.

Priest rubbed his jaw thoughtfully. "My team searched this entire floor but didn't find it. Maybe the killer took it with them."

"Or ate it."

"Or that."

"And you seriously think someone who works here could have done this?" Max gestured at the mutilated remains. "It looks like someone put him through a meat grinder."

"I don't know, Max. There are some pretty gifted agents on payroll. Merchants, shapeshifters, Kindred—do we really know exactly what any of them are capable of?"

"If that's your logic, then let's not ignore the fact that no one—myself included—knows exactly what freakish genome I belong to or what I'm capable of. Maybe I could have done this."

"First of all, you're not a freak. And secondly, I don't care what you are, there's no way you could have done this."

"Don't underestimate me, Priest. I could probably take you in a fight."

He chuckled. "Not a fair one."

"But all is fair in love and war," she quipped. Realizing the implication of her words, Max immediately wished she could take them back. She bit her lip. The intensity of Priest's gaze became unbearable.

"I'll keep that in mind," he said simply and walked to the door to hold it open. "Let's get you cleared through interviews. You're hunting with me tonight."

Six

The "interview" turned out to consist of Max being strapped to a lie detector and asked a series of control questions before a member of Priest's unit determined if she had a legitimate alibi, nurtured any ill-will toward the director, or knew of anyone who did. After that barrel of fun was over, she was transferred to an office converted to a clean room—covered and draped in plastic—where her hair and nails were thoroughly inspected for evidence. Then two of Priest's goons indicated that Max was to disarm and strip in order for her clothing and skin to be fully examined. It was around that time when Max's will to comply reached its limit.

They insisted, repeatedly. She refused…repeatedly. The soldiers were about three seconds from pulling their side arms when Priest entered the room with an expression similar to the one he wore yesterday morning when he had first stormed into her apartment.

"Hauser. Grey. That's enough."

"Sir," one of them said, turning to his attention to Priest but keeping one hand resting on his weapon, "the subject is refusing to complete her interview."

"I said that's enough," Priest growled in a dangerously low voice. "This goddamn interview is over."

"Yes, Sir."

"Give me the room," Priest commanded quietly. His tone hadn't changed.

"Yes, Sir," the soldiers replied in unison and saluted Priest.

As they cleared out, he turned stiffly to Max, still looking pretty pissed.

"Did you order that?" she asked before he could say anything. Her voice was trembling, and Max was so angry she couldn't stop it.

Clenching and unclenching his jaw, he shook his head. "Yes and no. The strip searches are supposed to be voluntary. As another option, we have a Level One who can detect the presence of Cranke's DNA using alternate methods."

"Am I supposed to report there now?"

"No." He exhaled a long breath. "This was just for the books. You're not a suspect. I was in a different room and didn't know those idiots would go so far." His right hand balled into a fist. "I'm so sorry, Max. This isn't like before. I said I'd never hurt you again, and I meant it."

"I believe you." The words had simply tumbled out, surprising Max, but she would have to beat herself up about that later. Right now, her hands were shaking with rage, and she couldn't see straight. She was afraid to think about what would've happened if Priest hadn't come in when he had.

"Thank you."

"No need." She concentrated on slowing her breathing and hoped her pulse would naturally follow. "It is what it is."

"The thank you was for not maiming my men." He took her hand, as his mouth curled into a gentle smile. He was relaxed, and that helped relax her.

"Oh yeah, then you should definitely thank me."

His thumb made a slow circle in her palm, then gradually applied pressure at the center. Max felt the final tendrils of rage retracting from her body, leaving her calm.

"What now?" she asked, her voice sounding normal again.

"Well, I told you about the Level One we have on staff." Priest still held her hand, leisurely moving his finger across the surface of her skin. Now that she was safely away from the edge, Max found it incredibly difficult to focus on what he was saying. "They can be frightening to some," Priest continued. "But I think you'll be okay."

Clearing her throat, Max withdrew her hand from his grasp. "So, this little interrogation by your merry men isn't over then?"

"You misunderstand me, Max. The Level One has identified the scent of whatever made a snack out of your boss and will be hunting with us."

*

Standing on the sidewalk next to a fully shifted Level One was a surreal experience. Unlike creatures from dimensional rifts, Level Ones were of this world. Formed from an entirely different genetic pool as the Kindred, Level Ones were essentially real-life versions of what myths and folklore considered werewolves. These creatures were rare, elusive, temperamental, and, for the most part, hated humans.

It was by means of DNA taken from these creatures and injected into human fetuses that genetically superior individuals like Arabella came to be. Several of the soldiers in Priest's unit were developed from a similar, but weaponized version of the program—code named "White Tree." Through White Tree, soldiers had attained watered down versions of a werewolf's natural abilities—supernatural hearing and smell, along with increased reflexes and strength. No one knew exactly how werewolves had evolved into existence, but it didn't take a genius to hypothesize why they hated humans so much.

Max had spent enough time in man-made cages being subjected to painful, invasive experiments that no normal human could survive—all for the purpose of military and scientific advancement. Staring into the Level One's eyes, she shivered at the amount of fury contained within them. Not because it was frightening, but because Max could identify with that rage.

"How did you get him to work for you?"

"Him is actually a her." Priest gestured to the midnight-colored wolf. "Kuro, this is Max. Max, this is Kuro."

The wolf sniffed the air in Max's direction, sat on her haunches and then turned her head away as if completely disinterested. Priest grinned. "She likes you."

Max studied the werewolf uncertainly. "How can you tell?"

"She usually snarls."

"Okay then."

He pulled a small device from the breast pocket of his tactical vest. "We'll move when you're ready, Kuro."

The wolf aimed a cool, yellow stare at them before climbing to her feet.

"Alright then." Taking Max by the elbow, Priest led her to a row of large, black SUVs parked curbside. Preoccupied with the handheld device the entire time, he guided Max to the passenger side of one of the vehicles. "Get in," he said.

Once they were both settled, Priest mounted the device to the dashboard. There Max could see a small blue dot blinking on an otherwise dark monitor. It was a tracker of some sort. Kuro must have been implanted with a subcutaneous GPS beacon because she certainly hadn't been wearing a collar. Underneath all that fur lived a human—at least part-time. Somehow it didn't seem right that she had been tagged like wildlife.

Her expression must have revealed her thoughts because Priest sighed. "No need to get all righteous with me, Max. You're preaching to the choir." He held up his forearm. "I have an implant too. Just like Kuro. A year ago, Command decided it needed to know where their assets were at all times."

Max felt a rush of heat flood through her face and neck. She knew all too well about Priest's origins. Sure, he had been conceived and born in a lab without parentage, designed only to be a living, breathing weapon. But many years had passed since then with Priest proving time and time again that he was a free thinking, free willed being. He was as human as anyone else. And no one, not the government, Global Cures, or the UCC had any right to deem otherwise.

"You're not their property."

Priest activated the turn signal before making a left onto a highway that would take them out of the city. A lull of silence followed, filled only by the sound of tires moving over faded asphalt. His tone was matter of fact. "You and I both know that's not true."

Reining in her temper, Max bit her tongue. It was an old argument between them. Priest would always be duty bound. The trait was practically hardwired into his nature. He didn't care how he was treated. Or what he lost. Max, of course, stood firm on the opposite side of that.

"How did Kuro—a werewolf—end up working for the UCC?" she asked instead, remembering Priest had avoided answering earlier.

"Are you sure you wanna know? Because you're definitely not going to like the answer."

"In order to keep something as fierce as a natural born werewolf on a leash, I know it would have to be pretty awful. Just tell me."

Priest cut his eyes at her, obviously still hesitant to reveal the truth. He murmured something under his breath before finally answering. "Kuro's pups are being held at a Global Cures facility. As long as she cooperates, they won't be subjected to testing or experiments…or otherwise destroyed."

Max's eyes widened with disbelief. "Priest! How could you?"

"Whoa. No." He shook his head emphatically. "I have nothing to do with the terms of Kuro's contract." Pausing to check the trajectory of the blinking dot, he pressed harder on the accelerator. "If I did, we couldn't work together. She isn't allowed within five hundred yards of the people responsible for holding her pups. Otherwise, things would get bloody real fast."

Max gritted her teeth. "The UCC is full of bastards. Sometimes, I hate myself for working for them."

"Good thing your daddy issues are stronger than your self-loathing. Otherwise, we wouldn't have gotten to spend all of this quality time together."

"That's not funny, Priest."

"I know." He lightly bumped her thigh with his fist. "C'mon. At least belonging to Marshal Services affords you some shielding. Until tonight, you didn't have to deal directly with any of Command's bullshit." He winked. "Imagine how dirty those pretty hands of yours would be if you were on my team."

"They'd be filthy," she agreed dryly.

"Love it when you talk dirty to me, baby."

Max rolled her eyes, but spared a small smile. Priest was trying to lighten the mood, and she appreciated that. It was better for the mission if she wasn't preoccupied with guilt by association in keeping Kuro's family captive. "You just passed the blue dot."

"Shit." Priest slammed on brakes. He eyed the monitor. "What the hell? She doubled back."

Max raised a wary eyebrow. "Do werewolves get confused often?"

He shrugged. "Am I a werewolf expert now?"

"Just drive." Falling silent, she let him dedicate his full concentration to the blinking blue dot, now moving almost erratically across the screen. Priest turned off the highway and ten minutes later, they were cruising through a disturbingly familiar neighborhood. Tension practically rolled off of his shoulders in visible waves. His jaw was rigid, but he didn't speak.

"Don't go getting all worked up," Max urged him. "This could just be a coincidence."

"I don't believe in coincidences."

Max sighed. "Right."

She couldn't make any more objections because the blue dot had stopped moving. Unfortunately, it's location was now right outside of the apartment complex where she lived. *Priest is right,* she thought. *This isn't good.*

Putting the SUV in park, he turned a grave stare in her direction. "If I tell you to wait here, are you going to try and hit me?"

"Damn right."

"You could be a target, Max."

She stuck her chin out. "Well, I'm not an easy target."

"No," he agreed, sliding out of the driver's seat and stepping into the night. "You've never been easy."

"You really want to drag our relationship issues into this right now?" Max shook her head, following him up the walkway. "Unbelievable." Swinging around as she heard a noise, her hand automatically went to the revolver at her hip.

Priest touched her shoulder. "Easy there, Sundance."

A figure stepped from the shadows and into the dim light of a nearby street post. If woodland fairies were real, and one of them happened to end up strung out and wandering the city streets, the woman standing on the sidewalk looked exactly how Max imagined a homeless, substance-addicted, woodland fairy would appear. She was on the shorter side, gauntly muscled, and with jet black, unruly hair adorned by several leaves and twigs. Unnaturally still, the woman scrutinized Max with eyes so piercing in intensity, they seemed feral.

"That's Kuro," Priest said needlessly, for Max had already made the connection.

The Level One walked toward them, those untamed brown orbs darting in all directions.

When she spoke, her voice was sharp with anger. "I lost the killer's trail."

Priest didn't sound happy either. "How could you have lost the trail? I can't imagine anything fooling that nose of yours unless whatever we're hunting can vanish into thin air."

Kuro shrugged. Though she addressed Priest, her unsettling gaze remained on Max. "The trail disappeared."

"Perfect." He studied the ten-story apartment building, looming like a beacon into the night sky. "So why did you bring us here then?"

"Because she needs to be here."

"That doesn't make any sense. What's here?"

"I'm not exactly sure."

"Is it the killer?"

"I don't think so."

"You're going to have to do better than that, Kuro."

For the first time, the she-wolf's wild stare shifted to Priest. She considered him for a long time before answering. "I'm not here to do the job for you, Harry." Then she brushed past him—all five feet and two inches of wild child—and headed straight into Max's apartment building.

Without a word, Max turned to follow, trying to resist the growing tightness in her chest, telling herself what had happened just now didn't matter and that if it did, she was an idiot. It was more important to find out why the werewolf thought it so pressing to abandon the hunt and take them back to Max's apartment. Who or what was here?

She was still on the sidewalk when Priest grabbed her arm. Snatching away, Max kept walking. "I don't care, Priest. Who you decide to fuck stopped being my business a long time ago."

"Then why are you pissed?"

"I'm not pissed. And this is not the time or place for this conversation."

"Max, it's not—"

"Seriously, Priest. Shut up so we can do the job we came to do."

"She's feisty," Kuro said. Wearing an impassive expression, she stood waiting just inside the doorway with her arms folded. "I see why you love her."

Hearing her words, ice water shot through Max's veins. Priest glowered at the she-wolf. "Thanks a lot, Kuro."

"No problem. Can we go upstairs now? This scent is odd and thick. It's driving me a little crazy."

"Lead the way," he said, still scowling.

As they climbed the stairwell, Priest refused to look at Max. She knew because she watched him the entire time. Kuro's words kept playing through her head. What exactly was between him and the werewolf? He certainly hadn't denied having sex with her. And did Max really care? Was it jealousy that spurted up, hot and sharp, when Kuro had addressed Priest with such familiar terms? People rarely called him Harrison, and never Harry. Max wanted to slam her own head against a wall. *Stop it.*

Jerking her brain away from the matter of Priest's sex life—which Max decisively assured herself that she did not care about—she directed her focus to the fact that Kuro had stopped right outside of her apartment door.

"And the plot thickens," she muttered.

"This isn't a joke, Max," Priest said in a terse whisper. "I can smell it now too, and I don't know what the hell it is. But you know what I do smell? Blood. Lots of it. Some of it belongs to your now deceased director."

"You know I had nothing to do with Cranke's murder."

"Command may not think so." Priest's lips pressed into a grim line as he pulled out his sidearm. "Kuro, get outside and cover the back."

Max drew her revolver. "Do you want the key, or do you plan on kicking my door in?"

After he nodded, she inserted her key into the lock as quietly as possible and turned the knob, wincing as she carefully pushed open the door and hoped the hinges didn't squeak. Max remembered being in bed just before getting the call to report to USPMS, and was certain she would have heard some creep sneaking around inside of her apartment. Whatever happened had transpired only after she had left for the agency, and after the director was already dead.

She cautiously poked her head inside. Kuro hadn't seemed too worried that the scent actually belonged to Director Cranke's killer, but Max couldn't be too careful. Single-handedly taking on a maddened kapre was all the excitement she needed for one weekend. Besides, the director had been a capable man, but whatever attacked him was clearly stronger and deadlier. Taking a deep breath, Max realized she was grateful to have Priest next to her.

Clearing the apartment would've have gone faster had they separated, but Priest insisted on keeping Max at his side as they moved from room to room. Living area, kitchen, guest bedroom, hall bathroom—all were clear. But with every room that didn't unveil the source of the strange scent Kuro had followed, the tension between Priest's shoulders only set in deeper. The rest of him, however, was the picture of calm. Soon, only Max's bedroom remained.

She had half a mind to be embarrassed by the dirty underwear, bras, and assorted clothing strewn about. She hadn't quite gotten around to doing the laundry...or washing the dishes, emptying the garbage, and going to the supermarket. The list went on. But Priest had already seen the disarray when he'd barged in on her yesterday morning, and Kuro was outside.

Moving to the right of the main bedroom door, Priest gestured for Max to hang back. She almost missed his signal as her attention was drawn to the bloody handprint smeared across white-trim of the doorframe, more blood that was still wet on the knob, and greyish black chunks of only-god-knew-what clinging within the smudge of crimson.

Pulling a glove from his back pocket, Priest folded a latex barrier around the knob and turned. It was unlocked. Though she had left a bedside lamp on earlier, no light came from beneath the door. Max's heart thudded in her ears, but beneath that sound, she could hear faint noises coming from within. Dramatic slurps and smacking as if someone were enjoying a giant bowl of ramen. A sickening feeling settled in Max's stomach.

When Priest clicked on his flashlight and shone it into the darkness, two shining orbs reflected back, disappearing briefly and then reappearing. The slurping paused and then resumed. Priest slowly moved the light to the source of the disturbing sound, and Max followed the beam's luminance, making out darkly colored circles beneath sunken eyes that shone out from a layer of leathered, sallow skin. A mouth rimmed in blood was surrounded by charred lips, stretched thin over several rows of very pointed teeth. The creature wore a collared shirt with copious stains of blood covering the pink cotton material. Max's eyes hesitantly fell to its pale and sharply clawed hands, busy picking and pulling at a dark, bloody object. Thankfully, Priest moved the light no further.

Swearing under his breath, he swiftly stepped into the room. Max gritted her teeth and followed.

"Put it down," Priest ordered. "Stand up slowly."

The smacking noises continued as the creature ignored them, continuing on as if they didn't even exist. Max's gaze flicked to the light switch and then back to the thing. There'd been barely any food to eat in the entire apartment, especially nothing to warrant this sort of feast. Maybe this creature had found the doggie bag containing the leftover steak dinner. Even as Max had the thought, she knew it foolish. No steak dinner was rare enough to produce so much blood. The gruesome showing before them would have necessitated at least half a cow.

A gut-churning snap originated from the creature's continued efforts to disassemble the bloodied object. Then it raised something to its mouth, with dark strands hanging from the gruesome fragment. Muted crunching followed as those needle-sharp teeth tore into flesh and bone.

Priest called her name in a low voice. "I want you to count to three and hit the lights. Be prepared for whatever happens next, but use non-lethal force."

Settle, Max told herself. *Settle.* Then she counted to three.

The room flooded with light, and the creature let out the most horrendous wailing screech that reached directly into Max's ears and stabbed through her skull with a metal spike. A bile-inducing splat sounded as the creature dropped the horrid thing it had been feasting upon. Momentum carried the misshapen ball a short distance towards Max's feet, and just like that, Director Cranke's missing head was recovered. Torn and partially skinned. Sockets emptied of eyeballs. The late director's skull was ripped open and his brain matter all but picked clean. There was barely time to process any of this because the creature was lunging toward Max in a blur of movement. Even as fast as it moved, she could have easily fired a shot, but instinctively, Max hesitated. A second before the monstrous thing slammed into her, she grappled for its shoulder, nearly recoiling at the feel of the malleable and leathered skin. Pivoting toward the creature, Max planted her feet wide and threw its weight forward, executing a throw that sent it sailing into the living room and crashing into the sofa. The creature flashed to its feet, rising to its full height as it let loose another brain-bleeding wail. It really was a ghastly thing. Dull grey skin wrapped tightly around a skeletal frame so thin that its clothing hung from the body. Bald, except for a few tufts of scraggly white hair, a severe underbite exposed several bottom rows of teeth and the raw gum line they protruded from. And the stench. The stench was awful.

Unleashing a fit of hisses and growls, the creature lowered its head, and its thin frame bobbed slowly from side to side as its black eyes gleamed, sizing them up. Then it attacked.

From beside Max, the sound of Priest's gun exploded. The creature dodged left, but a well of bluish-colored blood bubbled forth as the bullet tore a plug from its shoulder. Time slowed as Priest took aim again—as steady as a calm sea— even as the snarling beast charged toward them. Then things clicked into place as Max's brain solved the reason for her hesitation. The pink shirt. The dress slacks. This creature wore the very outfit Cute Kevin had on earlier that night at the agency when he had appeared so shaken about Director's Cranke's murder.

Throwing her hands up, Max knocked Priest's arm up and away, sending the round he fired into ceiling. Then she threw all of her weight into him, shoving him out of the creature's path as they tumbled together to the carpet.

"It's Kevin," Max said urgently. "Don't hurt him."

And then she rolled because the beast was on top of them. Grasping the collar of the bloodied pink shirt and the creature's shoulder, she planted her boot into its stomach, driving it up and overhead. This time, the kitchen's tiny island bar suffered through the creature's landing. Max pulled herself into a low crouch, barely registering a stinging pain in her left arm. Next to her, Priest had climbed to his feet and holstered his sidearm. A low growl slid from his throat as he met the creature's next charge.

It was over in seconds.

Ducking a swipe of the thing's razor-sharp claws, Priest slammed his fist into the side of its neck, hammering down on a bulging artery. Stunned by the blow, the creature staggered but then whipped its head around, snapping at Priest with needled teeth. Efforts rewarded with an elbow to the temple, the creature sagged, dropping half a foot down to Priest's height. Then he was wrapping it up, entangling its arms as his own hands squeezed the wretched thing's neck, applying pressure to the already damaged artery.

Its snarling gradually subsided and then altogether ceased. When Priest released his hold, it fell like a sack of bricks. He nudged it with his foot to make sure it was down. When nothing happened, Max hurried to his side.

Blood trickled from the creature's mouth and formed a small pool in the carpet beneath the shoulder. More concerning was its strained breaths, shallow and barely visible.

"You call that *not* hurting him?"

"I barely scratched him. He should be as good as new in a few hours." Priest knelt next to her, eyeing her injured arm worriedly. "You okay?"

Max glanced down. "That's nothing." Testing the arm, she winced. "I can barely feel it."

He nodded but that radioactive gaze continued to study her. "Nice moves."

"Thanks."

At last, Priest directed his attention to the unconscious creature. "You got any rope?"

Max smiled. "No. But I have handcuffs…and duct tape."

Seven

Despite her objections, Priest insisted on treating her shoulder with antibiotic salve and then dressed the wound with a bandage. He worked mostly in silence, concentrating on his task. His hands were warm, his touch tender, and Max was keenly aware of each moment when his fingertips brushed against her skin. Shivering, she tried focusing her thoughts elsewhere. Examining her co-worker's bruised neck and bloodied shoulder did well to distract her. It was a stern reminder of the violence those gentle hands were capable of.

Handcuffed and duct taped to the kitchen chair, Kevin was completely human and still unconscious. About twenty minutes post-knockout, his monstrous form had given way to pink flesh, normal teeth, and a full head of handsome hair. Max was grateful for it. Cute Kevin was cute again.

Finishing his work, Priest closed the first aid kit and pushed it to the side of the table.

"You know you didn't have to do that," Max said, referring to her body's accelerated ability to heal itself as she shrugged her jacket back on.

"Maybe I just like taking care of you."

Sighing, she turned away from him. "Stop doing that."

"Doing what?"

"You know what I'm talking about."

"Pretend I don't. See if we're on the same page."

Max folded her arms. The resolute set of Priest's jaw told her that he wasn't going to let it go. She decided to forge the path of least resistance and play along. "You've been relentless these past thirty-six hours, but you don't have to be. I'm not dead, and I don't plan on dying anytime soon. So, please go back to being the estranged ex-lover who only comes around when Daddy sends him to fetch me."

"That's how you see this."

"Yes."

"Wow." Priest drew one hand across his face. "Did you hear none of what I said to you at the gala?"

"Hearing and believing are two very different things."

"Well, believe it. I never got over you, Max."

She snorted. "The Level One downstairs whose legs you're crawling between proves otherwise."

"So, you are angry about that."

Damn it. Of course, it was easy to see through her if she was going to be transparent. "I'm only making a point."

"I haven't touched her in six months."

"I think she wants you to touch her now."

"Goddammit, Max." Priest exhaled forcefully through his nostrils. "Stop making this into something it's not. I messed up a great thing, and I was trying and failing to live with it. Kuro and I were two rage-filled fuck-ups who fell in the sack together a few times. It was just sex. There is nothing there. You're still the only one for me."

"Okay." Max cleared her throat. Heat pooled into her face and swept over the rest of her body. Continuing the conversation was a rabbit hole she didn't want to venture into. She could be honest and admit to him that she'd never gotten over him either. But then where would that lead? She was afraid to think about it. "Let's talk about something else."

The chair scraped heavily against the floor as Priest shoved back from the table and stood up. Pacing in silence, he kept his head down but every now and then those blue eyes would glance at her and flash with anger. Eventually, his pacing came to a halt, followed by a muted sigh. When he spoke again, the fury was gone, and his tone was all business. "How long have you known that your friend is a wendigo?"

"I had no idea."

"I'm not sure I believe that."

126

"You think I'm a liar, then."

A familiar honey-coated drawl intercepted whatever reply Priest had in mind. "Holy shit, you two have issues." Fully awake, Kevin spat a mouthful of blood onto the kitchen floor. Max grimaced. The damage done to her apartment tonight was beyond her skill set. Maybe she should hire a maid service. As if she could afford it.

"Max is telling the truth," Kevin continued, coming to her defense. "She had no idea what I am. Though now she probably understands how I know all of her secrets," he finished with a devilish wink and a bloodstained smile.

Sorting through a mental rolodex of info about the paranormals that migrated across the rifts, Max made the connection. "Wendigos are mind readers."

"Well, not all of us, sweetheart. But it certainly helps with the hunt." He looked pointedly at the bindings around his chest, legs, and arms. Max had used up two rolls of duct tape to properly secure him. One was of the traditional matte grey and the other was patterned in pink camouflage. "Is all this really necessary?"

Priest was unsympathetic. "You broke into Max's apartment. We found you on her bed, eating the director's severed head. And then you attacked us."

"Oh," Kevin said simply and swallowed. "Right."

"We gotta ask," Max began, needing to hear it directly from Kevin that one of her closest friends wasn't actually a murderer. "Did you kill the director?"

"No," he said quickly. "Director Cranke was already dead when I got there, and the doors were sealed. The security system wasn't even triggered. I know that probably looks bad because I have access but so do about two dozen other people." Eyes widening, Kevin's voice thinned with anxiety. "Please believe me. I didn't murder him."

"Kevin," Max said gently. "Start from the beginning. Tell us exactly what happened when you got to the agency."

"And what you were doing there in the first place," Priest added.

"I was there because the director called me. Working the crowd at the gala and kissing the mayor's ass had him stressed. He wanted to blow off some steam."

"Wait," Max said, reading between the lines. "So, you and the director?" She laughed. "Kevin and Kevin? That's cute. All the shit you know about my life and you didn't tell me this."

"It was really nothing to tell, Max. Cranke and I hooked up from time to time, but he had a girlfriend. He was committed to her."

Max lifted one eyebrow. "Hooking up with you is a funny way of showing commitment to his girlfriend."

"Please don't get her started," Priest interjected. "What happened after you arrived at the agency?"

"Like I said, the doors were sealed, but that wasn't unusual. Nothing was out of place, that is until I used my code to bypass security. As soon as the doors opened, I knew something was wrong. The smell of blood was everywhere, but that wasn't all. The heart, liver, and intestine—to wendigo, these organs have a very distinctive smell. Standing in the corridor, I could sense them all. I knew the director was dead before I ever set foot in his office."

"Why didn't you call the police?" Priest asked.

Kevin blushed, avoiding their gazes when he answered. "For someone like me, the smell of a fresh kill can be overpowering—irresistible to a starving wendigo. Understand this—I am a scavenger. I don't kill humans. Before tonight, my last meal was a month ago when I came across a hooker who had been beaten to death. After smelling what was basically a buffet to wendigo senses, I went into the director's office, drawn like a bee to a wildflower. The last thing I remember thinking was something had torn him up pretty good. I must have gone into some kind of feeding frenzy because I lost all sense of time. For a while, I even forgot where I was. When I came to again—well there was a lot less evidence left. Oh man." Kevin choked on a sob. "I can't believe I ate him. He was a friend. A decent boss and a great lay…and I ate him."

Max squeezed his uninjured shoulder, offering what little comfort she could. "He was already dead, Kevin. And you were starving. What choice did you have?"

Inconsolable, Kevin sobbed again. "I could have not eaten my friend."

"Hey," Priest said with surprising gentleness. "This moment won't seem so bad later when you're sitting on the toilet and realize that the shit coming out of your ass is actually a former lover."

Max glared at Priest and had never wanted to hit him so badly in her life. But then Kevin barked a laugh and finally looked at them again. Some tears lingered in his eyes, but the self-loathing was mostly gone. "That's really twisted, man," he said.

A smile hinted at Priest's lips. "It's all about perspective." He grew serious again. "Why did you come here, Kevin? And why bring the head?"

"Max said she would find me later, and I really needed to explain to someone what happened. I couldn't speak up at the agency because I knew I would sound guilty as hell, especially after people learned what I am. No offense, but you ghosts aren't exactly a forgiving bunch. As for the head, it was already here. Just sitting on your bed, Max." He shrugged in a defeated manner. "I was still hungry. I'm not proud of it."

Taking a step back, Max cut her eyes at Priest. That one vein was protruding from the side of his neck.

Whoever had killed the director had been inside of her apartment, and they had left a bloody, severed head on top of her only comforter. It was clearly a message. But why?

Grabbing a knife from the kitchen drawer, Max cut Kevin's bindings. It was clear that he was fully in control of himself and meant them no harm. Priest must have agreed, because he didn't object or try to stop her.

Hands freed, Kevin leaned forward in the chair and rubbed the bruises on his neck. "What now?"

Max deferred to Priest. His standing in the UCC far outranked her position as a marshal, and technically, this was his investigation. She knew she had no say in what would become of her friend, and therefore was completely caught off guard by Priest's answer.

"What happens to you now depends on Max."

"Okay then," she said, recovering quickly. "Let him go. We know he had nothing to do with Director's Cranke's death."

"Not so fast." Priest moved closer to her, wearing an alarmingly determined expression. "Whoever or whatever brutally murdered your boss knows exactly where you live and made it a point to leave a severed head on your bed. You can't stay here, Max. This place is compromised."

Max nodded. She saw no reason to argue with that. "I'll go to Arabella's."

"No."

"What do you mean, no?"

"Arabella is good, but she's no match for this. I want you to remain with me tonight."

"At your place? No way." Max couldn't even contemplate it. There wasn't enough will power in the world to ensure her survival if she spent a night alone with Priest.

"You agreeing to this is the only scenario where your friend walks away free."

"Damn you, Priest." Her voice trembled with anger. "This is low, even for you."

His hand whipped out in a flash of movement before she could even think to react. "Maxima,'" he said, lightly cupping her cheek against his palm. "I'd kneel in hell if it meant keeping you safe."

Max didn't know what to say. She was furious at him for taking away her choice in the matter, essentially extorting her to achieve the outcome he wanted. Priest damn well knew she wouldn't sacrifice Kevin just to have her way. He was controlling her life, just like her father. And just like her father, she both hated and loved him equally.

"Damn," Kevin exclaimed, fanning himself in an exaggerated manner. "Sweetheart, if you won't spend the night with him, I will."

*

Less than an hour later, Max found herself in Priest's townhouse, sitting on a bed in the second-level guestroom and wearing one of his t-shirts. Max was a tall girl, but Priest's flawlessly constructed physique still towered over her. Any of his shirts were easily large enough to cover all of her important bits.

Carefully removing the pins from her wig, she tossed it onto a bedside table. Then she loosened the band holding back her mane of curls. She shook her head, sending thick, golden hair tumbling to her shoulders. *Free at last.*

Max dug into the small overnight bag she'd packed before leaving her apartment. After wresting her cooperation to come here, Priest had at least allowed her a few moments to gather some things (but nothing from the bedroom because everything there was to be processed by a forensic team) before ushering her downstairs to the SUV. He'd kept his word and let Kevin go, but with one caveat. In the morning, Kevin would have to formally register with the proper authorities as an otherworldly species crossed over from a rift, turning over an exact date and coordinates for his migration to the human world.

It was certainly better than the alternative, but Max still felt sad for him. Anonymity was a precious thing for someone who wasn't completely human. From now on Kevin would be watched—carefully—because wendigo were dangerous creatures. She hoped he would somehow be able to keep his job at the Paranormal Marshal Services, but knew it was unlikely.

When her search failed to uncover a toothbrush, Max muttered a curse. She sat at the edge of the bed for a moment, chewing a fingernail and deliberating. Making a decision, she stood again and walked down the short hallway to the master bedroom, where she found the door open and a freshly showered Priest. A light grey towel was wrapped about his waist, leaving his rippled torso bare and slick with beads of moisture. His blond hair stood atop his head in wet spikes, slightly darkened by its dampness. The black and grey scene of the native warrior battling a towering demon within a harsh landscape came to life as his back and shoulders rippled with movement. A dragon's tail spilled into the fight, adding a sort of juxtaposition between real life and fantasy. Just as in their world, that line was becoming more and more blurred with each day, and with every new species that passed through the rifts.

Knowing there was precious little time to admire the view before Priest sensed she was there, she let her eyes roam freely across his exposed body. It came as a jolt of surprise to Max, realizing how much she actually wanted to touch him. Feeling guilty, she chewed her lip. Was it really so bad to admit—if only to herself—that she missed him? As a nagging feeling of déjà vu descended upon her, the towel dropped to the floor, and Max's thoughts were scattered beyond recovery.

Except for an odd symbol on Priest's right calf and the depiction of a prowling, winged lion with large and curved horns on its head and tail of a serpent that snaked high up his left leg, the tattoos stopped at his waist. Max now got a nice side view of that drawing and everything else— Priest's tight ass, well-defined thighs, and the ample package that hung between them. Heat rising to her face, Max bit her lip harder.

"Are you going to stand there, ogling me all night," Priest asked as he turned to face her, giving Max the full-frontal view. "Or are you going to come in?" On seeing her expression, he broke into a wide grin.

Her blush intensified and Max could do nothing to stop it. She felt like an idiotic school girl. It was beyond her why the lab geeks at Global Cures had found it necessary to bestow genetically engineered super soldiers with perfect cocks.

Clearing her throat, she forced her gaze upward and locked them onto Priest's electric eyes. "I forgot my toothbrush."

"There might be an extra one around here someplace." Strolling casually into his bathroom as if his godlike physique wasn't on stark display, Priest came back with a packaged toothbrush, and offered it to Max while still wearing that wicked grin and nothing else.

She snagged the toiletry. "Thanks," she said and rapidly retreated, moving away from the magnetism of his body.

Back to safety in the guestroom, Max closed the door and clutched the toothbrush against her chest. She took a deep breath. *Shit. Shit. Shit.*

If it was possible for a million things to run through the brain at once, that phenomenon was happening at that very moment. Her sense of self-preservation ordered her to grab her things and run out of Priest's townhouse as fast as she could, putting as much distance between her and her ex-boyfriend as their mutual zip code would allow. No matter the intent or how sincere the apology, their relationship had ended because she had trusted Priest, and he had returned that trust by locking her in a cage for three days while scientists poked and prodded her body during a non-stop succession of tests. She couldn't give him a second chance. She just couldn't. Max closed her eyes.

But before then, things with Priest had been better than any girl could hope for. Sure, they'd fought as much as they made love, but that was because they were each other's equal in every sense of the word. In truth, Priest was everything Max wanted. Perhaps that was why getting over him had been impossible.

It was then that her heart and brain clicked into alignment. Terrified and exhilarated all at once, Max gradually accepted the decision. Setting the toothbrush aside, she opened the bedroom door and stepped into the hallway. Instantly, she smacked into Priest's chest. At least he was wearing clothes this time.

Taking Max by the shoulders, he helped steady her. "Now where are you going in such a hurry?"

Glaring up at him, she immediately couldn't answer. After roughly a year of denying her feelings, while trying and failing to move past the obstacle that was Priest, Max—in an act that went against all laws of self-preservation—had finally torn down the dam. The emotions that rushed in were paralyzing.

"Hey," Priest said more gently as his eyes narrowed with concern. "Is everything okay? Your heart is racing."

She shook her head. "Where were you going just now?" Even to her own ears, her tone was bitchy enough to put Priest on the defensive.

"I live here, Max. I can go where I want."

Repeating the question, she tried to soften her voice. "Where were you going, Priest?"

He sighed. "I was coming to apologize for making you uncomfortable earlier. I was out of line." He hesitated. "Especially after you agreed to come here tonight. I can't imagine how hard it must be for you." His gaze dropped to the carpeted floor. Even after all this time, shame weighed as heavily on Priest as betrayal had on Max.

Positioning herself so that their bodies were flush, she took his chin in her hand and pulled him down to her level. "Make me regret this, and I will kill you," she promised.

The way his face lit up with hopeful surprise nearly broke her heart, as did the moisture that filled his eyes just before he buried his head against her shoulder. The soldier designed to have no emotion, brought to tears by forgiveness. Max wanted to cry.

She laughed instead. "Pull yourself together and fuck me."

Priest lifted his face and, gripping both sides of her head, locked his gaze onto hers for several intense seconds. "Yes, ma'am," he whispered. Then he pressed his mouth into hers.

One kiss said everything between them that words could not. Grief, longing, sadness, bliss, resentment, and understanding passed from her mouth to his. Progressively, the tone shifted to something more passionate, becoming almost urgent as Max couldn't seem to get enough. His lips, his tongue, his teeth—she tasted it all. If she could have crawled inside of his skin, it would not have sated her.

She could tell Priest's craving for her was just as powerful from the way he stripped the borrowed shirt from her body before lifting her up and tossing her onto the bed. There, his mouth went to her breasts, kissing each mound, licking and sucking until her nipples were turgid with arousal. His tortuous kisses trailed down her abdomen, dipping into her navel, and still lower. Then his head was between her thighs, licking sweetly into her folds, making her gasp. His tongue circled her clit, even as his fingers pierced her, burrowing as deeply as they would go. Max moaned. She wanted—needed—more. She craved for him to be inside of her.

"Priest," she whispered. Clutching his shoulders as a wave of pleasure rolled over her, Max rocked her hips against his mouth, writhing uncontrollably against the sensations that coursed through every nerve ending in her body. Her breaths quickened. Her stomach twitched and trembled, curling toward the ecstasy centered between her legs. And then that center broke, spreading outward to envelop her in a dizzying rapture that left Max panting for air.

She stared at the ceiling, still twitching with aftershocks, and felt his weight lift from the bed. She heard his clothing tossed to the floor, and then his naked body was on top of hers, his weight offset by his muscled biceps on either side of her. Max spread her knees, allowing him to settle between her legs while she admired how seamlessly they fit together. She had missed this so much.

Feeling his throbbing, engorged shaft press against her thighs, her eyes closed and a content smile curled at her lips. Max lifted her hips, encouraging him to dip inside of her, but he resisted, making her wait, adding fuel to the flames of her desire.

His hand slid across her belly and up to her breasts where he fondled and teased each nipple. Lowering his mouth to those dark little buds, he seared a trail to her neck, lavishing her skin with hot kisses. Her nails dug into his skin, as her fingers flexed and uncurled, while the rest of her body writhed beneath the pleasure of his merciless assault.

When Max was certain she couldn't bear it any longer, he at last entered her, impaling her body with a quick thrust of his hips. At first, she cried out sharply. Then her body adjusted to his wide girth, and she groaned each time he rocked forward, moving with his rhythm, urging him deeper, and begging him to fuck her harder.

He answered by stalling his movements, slowly withdrawing until only the very tip of him remained inside. Then he slowly pushed forward, sinking his massive cock into her womb. He did that, again and again, hitting all the right places to bring her to the brink of another release. Just as her body began to tense, tightening around the torture that pierced within her, he changed the momentum, ramming against her with violent, rapid thrusts. Pain became inseparably entwined with pleasure as her body endured the vigorous pounding. Then she broke, and Max screamed through the climax, vaguely aware of the moisture that spilled between her thighs.

Now it was Priest who moaned. "You're so fucking sexy," he whispered and kissed her. "One more time, Max. Do it with me."

Exhausted and trembling, Max didn't think it possible. But as his hips continued to surge against her, stroking her from deep within, her body slowly began to respond. And then she tightened down as much as she could, squeezing hard enough to stop his movement and trap him inside of her. That was all took. Face tightening, his abdomen rippled, and his body briefly stalled. Then Priest grunted as his hips jerked, reflexively pumping with his own release. Beneath him, Max was besieged by another cluster of spasms. Spent, with every muscle liquefied, she fell back limply against the bed. Max wasn't sure she could move again even if the house had burst into flames.

"That was amazing," she said, not too stingy to give credit where it was due.

Chuckling, Priest rolled to one side and pulled her against him. "Give me ten minutes, and we're doing that again."

Eight

It was just before dawn when Max stirred awake. There was an odd heaviness to the air and strange vibrating sensation moved across her skin. Lifting her head from Priest's chest, she whispered his name and nudged him awake. Tensing, he became instantly alert. Max gave him a questioning gaze, and he nodded.

"I hear it," Priest said softly.

She frowned. Max couldn't actually hear anything, but somehow knew something was there.

Priest pointed to the roof and slid from the bed. Max followed, wincing at the soreness between her legs. Moving quietly, she slipped on the borrowed shirt and the only pants she had. Priest pulled on pajama bottoms and extracted a handgun from a holster hidden beneath the nightstand as Max gathered her own weapons. Sheathing the Shrike tomahawk, she gripped the revolver in one hand. The weight of some other presence pressed in from all sides, squeezing Max with a sense of dread. She didn't know what it was, but it was here. And it was stalking them.

A sudden and loud *thunk* sounded from right over their heads, as if something had jumped or landed on top of the roof. There was a long stretch of silence, followed by a softer but methodic series of eerie thumps, punctuated by the sound of something heavy being dragged along behind.

Footsteps. Max was sure of it. Something was walking on Priest's roof. Something big and— she didn't know how she knew—something *ancient*. The footsteps abruptly ended, and Max took a deep breath. Hell was about to break loose.

The bedroom window shattered, exploding inward as if a massive thing had crashed through, but Max saw nothing. Then Priest opened fire, shooting an unseen target. Max re-focused her senses and thought a shadow moved near the window, but wasn't sure. As she took aim, a dull roar tore through the room, reaching down into her very bones to shake them, causing her to nearly drop the revolver. And then Priest was flying into the wall, hammered sideways by an invisible but powerful force. Dread solidified within her belly as Max considered whether another kapre had tracked her down to get vengeance for what she and Kali had done to Nihilson. But that was crazy. Tree giants never ventured so far outside of their territory and definitely not into crowded cityscapes.

Shoving the thought aside, Max watched Priest regain his footing only to be immediately knocked down again. She wanted to shoot, but couldn't see a thing now and feared putting a bullet into Priest instead of whatever it was that attacked him. Deciding the damn gun was useless, Max holstered it.

Suddenly, the pressure in the atmosphere intensified, moving toward her like a concussive wave, and Max acted purely on instinct. Grasping for the tomahawk, she thrust the steel head forward, and was surprised to connect solidly with the unseen entity. Max lashed out repeatedly, using a combination of cuts and chopping strikes, until she smelled blood and somehow sensed the creature's pain. The heaviness abated, but then a dull roar saturated the room again, and Max was blindsided by a clobbering blow to the head. First there were stars. And then as she fell, a combustion of light dazzled her eyes, momentarily robbing Max of all sight. While in that darkness, the entity's agony ripped through her like a heated blade. Then the light was gone, and Max could see it.

Biting back the scream that clawed at her throat, Max lifted both hands to protect herself, tasting her own blood as she did so. Speechless, she stared up at the monstrous creature, looming so tall that its gruesome head scraped the ceiling. Max had never seen anything like it and was certain her life was about to end. But then something amazing happened.

Her palms began to glow from within as golden light surrounded them, like a dim aura encircling the full moon. Rays of the same color stretched outward in thin, elongated streaks of light. And then there was a flash, overlaid by a muted boom as the golden rays erupted into a pulse that slammed into the monster, powerful enough to send it crashing backward into the opposite wall.

The heavy, pressing feeling dissipated.

The roaring stopped.

Max waited.

Both she and Priest wore matching expressions of bewilderment. Max was pretty certain the creature had gone, but still, she stood with Priest—watching and listening for any sign of further attack. Neither of them uttered a word, as if one sound would invite disaster.

After some time, it was Max who finally spoke. "I think it's gone."

Priest nodded. "Me too."

Then they rushed to each other, and Priest hugged Max hard enough to knock her off her feet, holding on as if he never wanted to let go. He kissed her hair and squeezed the back of her neck, while she rested her head against his chest, listening to the steady beating of his heart. Despite what had just happened, his pulse was as even as ever. In contrast, Max's heart pounded hard enough to burst from her chest.

"What the hell was that?" Even as she asked, Max wished she hadn't because the creature's terrifying appearance came rushing back to mind.

"I don't know. Maybe we just had our first run in with Director Cranke's murderer." Priest pulled back to see her face. "I saw the way you fought. Could you see it?" he asked.

Max shook her head. "Not until you used those flash grenades. Why would that hurt it?"

"The grenade was actually a concentrated dose of ultraviolet light." Priest suddenly sounded weary as he leaned into her. "They were developed as a weapon against nocturnal species, since some sort of photosensitivity is usually involved." Taking a deep breath, he grimaced. "I need to sit."

Worried, Max hurriedly checked him over. Two large gashes lacerated his side, just beneath his ribcage. Helping Priest to the edge of the bed, she switched on a nearby lamp. The wounds were deep, completely splitting the top layer of skin and slicing into the fatty layer below. She was positive the injury must have hurt like hell, but nothing vital had been affected and the muscle damage was minimal. "You'll be fine in a day or two, but you're going to need stitches."

"Great," he muttered with absolutely no enthusiasm.

Wasting no time, Max went to retrieve the first aid kit. When she came back, Priest was on the phone with his people. He was mid-sentence, reporting the attack and explaining the possibility of it being the same creature responsible for Director Cranke's untimely demise, when Max pressed a towel to his wounds to slow the bleeding. Hissing, Priest fell silent. He closed his eyes and leaned away from her as if to escape the pain. Whoever was on the other end of the line called his name a few times. Taking a deep breath, Priest finished the briefing, issued a few succinct orders, and ended the call.

He glared at Max. "Ouch."

"We need to get this bleeding under control," she said. Taking note of his clenched fists and the way his eyes pinched together, she risked easing off the pressure in the slightest bit. "Think about something else. You were shooting before you used the UV grenades, before I could see anything. Could you see it then?"

"Sort of. But not if I looked directly at it…only in my peripheral."

Max chewed her lip. "Priest."

"Yeah."

She hesitated. If she had decided to trust him, then now was the moment. "I could sense it, Priest. That was why I woke up. I sensed the creature's presence—its power."

His gaze was unreadable. "And the light from your hands…I've never seen that ability in you before," he said after studying her for a quiet minute.

"That's new to me too. I don't know how I did it. After you used the grenades, I could see the thing. It was pure evil, Priest. Did you see it?"

He shook his head. "I didn't get a good look. From behind, it seemed reptilian."

"Or something." Max closed her eyes, and those hungry, soulless eyes loomed before her again, desperate to devour her. "It seriously freaked me out, Priest. The blast—pulse—or whatever just happened."

"I'm glad it did."

Max sighed. "You were right to ask to me to stay here tonight. I hate to think of what could have happened had I been at Arabella's instead."

Something between a grimace and a smile crossed his features. "Yeah, I probably handle getting my ass kicked a little better. How's your head? You took a pretty nice bump." He started to reach for her, but a grunt of pain eased from his lips and he bailed on the movement halfway.

"It's fine. Worry about yourself." She peered beneath the towel to check his wound. The blood flow had at least decreased to a slow ooze. "When will the medic get here?"

"Within the hour. They'll investigate the scene, collect evidence, and ask lots of questions." Jaw clenched, Priest looked away from her and seemed to be struggling with something. At last he spoke. "Don't tell anyone about the light from your hands or how you could sense the creature. I mean it, Max. Tell no one…not even your father."

*

Though the guest bedroom was wrecked, the rest of the house remained untouched. So, once the forensic team left, Max went to Priest's room and crawled into bed for a few more hours of shut eye. She had dutifully answered what felt like an endless barrage of questions, careful to omit any details alluding to her connection with the creature or the burst of power she'd manifested to eventually dispel it. But that was twice in one night her sleep had been interrupted, and two battles with two very different creatures. She was exhausted. Priest needed to wrap up a few more things, but had promised to join her upstairs. Waking up, Max wasn't sure he actually ever did. His side of the bed was undisturbed.

Yawning, Max rolled to her feet and shuffled to the bathroom. She took a quick shower and trimmed her nails. Then she went to the guestroom to retrieve her wig, toothbrush, and fresh contacts. The wig was ruined. Blood and shards of glass had made an unsalvageable mess of the once luxurious raven locks. Now the only thing the wig was fit for was the garbage.

Ugh.

Commandeering a tiny amount of Priest's hair gel, she attacked her golden curls with a stiff brush, fixing her own hair as best she could. Satisfied the frizz was mostly under control, Max tied her thick mane into a low bun and then went downstairs to find Priest. He was in the kitchen, busy at the stove with his back to her. From what was scattered across the countertop, Max surmised he was making a breakfast of pancakes, bacon, and scrambled eggs.

"You owe me a wig," she said, walking up behind him. "Between your blood and the broken glass, one of my favorite accessories is now useless to me. I'm forced to go au naturel today…with my hair that is," she amended, remembering that she at least had contacts to hide behind. "Hey," she said, when he didn't respond. "How are you feeling?"

No answer.

She touched his shoulder. "Priest?"

He finally turned, and Max choked back a scream.

His throat had been slashed, and the wound at his side appeared as if it had reopened, now encompassing his entire abdomen. So much blood saturated his shirt, Max didn't think it possible he had any left inside.

With shaking hands, she touched him. His skin was cold and ashen. His eyes—normally so bright and blue—were dulled and darkened as the light rapidly faded from them. Priest was looking right at her, but it seemed as if he didn't really see her. "Max, don't," he whispered. "Please. You have to go."

"Priest what happened? You need to sit down."

"No. Just go." His eyes rolled back until all the blue was gone and only the stark white of his corneas remained. As he sagged to the floor, Max caught him. She was confused and losing the fight against rising panic.

Max reached for her cell, but couldn't find it. She screamed a curse, then patted his face. "Stay with me, Priest. Stay with me." She was losing him. She could feel it. Terror squeezed her innards and Max swore again.

"Max?" A very puzzled sounding Priest called out to her from the kitchen doorway. "Who are you talking to?"

Max looked up and couldn't believe her eyes. It was Priest. Standing there, looking gorgeous in the morning sunlight…and completely unharmed. There was no blood. His skin wasn't pale. In fact, he was virtually glowing. Save for a little weariness around the eyes—probably from missing yet another night of sleep—he looked fine.

What the hell?

Max looked down. Her hands were empty. Priest wasn't dying on the kitchen floor.

"Max?"

She stood up. "Where were you just now?"

"I had to take a call from Captain Knox. She wanted updates on the investigation." He moved toward her cautiously, as if approaching a frightened animal. "You okay, Max? You sound really upset."

"Oh." Too many thoughts were in her head all at once, hurting her brain. Max didn't know what to think, what to feel, or what to believe. "I'm fine," she answered absently. Hurrying past him before he could ask another question, Max darted upstairs and snagged her overnight bag from the floor. She tore through its contents until she found the stash of pills, but just as she was about to open the bottle and take one, Priest snatched the entire thing from her hands.

A frown creased his forehead as he scanned the label. "Why are you taking these?"

"They're antipsychotics."

"I can read. I asked why you're taking them."

Max folded her arms. "Priest, give me the damn pills." To be honest, she wasn't entirely sure that she was even talking to an actual person. Although...the hallucinations so far were consistently of a bleeding, dying Priest.

However, both hallucinations had started out with a normal, non-bleeding or non-dying Priest.

"I'll give them back when you tell me why you're taking them."

"Dammit, Priest." He had to be real. Only the real Priest could be so infuriating. Max stared him down, but he wasn't budging. She couldn't wrestle with him to retrieve the bottle by force because the risk of tearing loose his stitches wasn't worth it. "Fine," she said, gritting her teeth. "After last year…once I was released…there were some issues." She paused, trying to find the right way to say it. Then Max threw her hands up. *Screw it.* "I lost my shit, okay? Nightmares, confusion, paranoia, voices that weren't there—the doctors called it psychosis. I couldn't tell what was real anymore, Priest. I thought you knew. Why else would my father insist on babysitters for his adult daughter?"

From the stricken look on his face, Max realized he hadn't known. "I knew you had some trouble adjusting," he started uncertainly, "but—"

"Anyway," Max said, cutting him off. "I think the hallucinations are coming back."

"Since when?"

Max shrugged. "Two days ago."

Priest closed his eyes and slowly reopened them. Then he finally relinquished the pill bottle.

She laughed bitterly. "Having second thoughts, now that I'm a certified lunatic?"

"Max, you were crazy when I met you. You just weren't medicated."

"And you were an asshole," she said, but flashed a genuine smile. "Too bad they don't make pills for that."

"Ouch." He clutched his chest dramatically, as if she had hurt him. "Well this asshole got up early to make you breakfast." He tugged at her hands, pulling her toward him.

"You got up early just for me?" Max repeated, infusing doubt in her words as she resisted his pull.

Priest looked toward the ceiling. "Okay, no. I never actually slept, but that doesn't lessen the effort that went into the banana chocolate pancakes that are waiting for us downstairs."

Her eyes widened. "Those are my absolute favorite." Laughing, Max gave up the struggle and fell into his arms. "Harrison Preesti, I take back just about all the awful things I've said about you."

Priest let out a chuckle of his own. "Come here," he said and kissed her slowly. He held her for moment longer, scrutinizing her with a serious gaze. "You're going to be okay, Max."

She hugged him, burying her face against his shirt. She wanted to believe him, but Max couldn't shake the feeling that something terrible was coming.

"Let's go have some those pancakes," she said. "See if you've lost your touch."

Turning her around, Priest herded her toward the stairs and smacked her ass. "I am the pancake king," he said, causing Max to burst into a fit of laughter.

Were it not for the fact that the compliment would have gone straight to his head, she would have conceded with Priest's boastful declaration because his pancakes turned out to be fluffy, golden, and buttery morsels of perfection. They chatted while they ate, keeping the conversation light and flirty. There seemed to be an unspoken, mutual agreement to avoid the subject of where things stood between them now that they had fallen in bed together again. Max dreaded having that inevitable conversation. Sure, she had decided to trust Priest, but it didn't mean Max wanted to be back in a full-blown relationship. She wasn't ready. And she suspected that Priest wasn't either.

After treating herself to a second helping of pancakes, Max thanked Priest for breakfast and shrugged into her jacket. It was Sunday—laundry day. She needed to get back to her apartment, assess the damage, find and hire a maid service if necessary. There was also the report that needed to be finished concerning Friday night's tree giant fiasco.

"Just where do you think you're going?"

"Back to my apartment. I've got work to do, Priest. I can't hide out here forever."

"First of all, you're not hiding. Secondly, you're with me today."

"I don't need a babysitter."

"That may be true, but I need you to identify what you saw last night."

"I already told you, I've never seen anything like it."

"Right." He stood from the table. "So, we're going to my office. Command keeps a catalogue of everything that's crossed over since the rifts started happening. Maybe we'll have some luck there."

Max crossed her arms. "If I help you I.D. this thing, will you let me go then?"

Priest spread his hands innocently. "You say that like I'm keeping you prisoner."

"I know you, Priest," she said, narrowing her eyes. "After what happened last night, you've already come up with a dozen different ways to keep me in your sights. And you probably have men assigned to track me when that's not possible."

He gathered their plates from the table as she spoke, dumping them into the sink. "You're wrong on that last part. None of my men are involved."

Max lifted an eyebrow but didn't say anything.

"You're going to love this," Priest said, but the roguish grin on his face inferred that Max would positively not love it. "Kuro has agreed to keep an eye on you and help out if there's any trouble."

"You ordered an indentured she-wolf to watch my back. That's comforting," Max said sarcastically.

"Wrong again." Priest leaned against the counter, wise to keep his distance. "Kuro actually volunteered for this assignment." He winked. "Maybe it's you who she wants to touch."

Getting the sense that he was only half-joking, Max tilted her head. "But you and her were a thing."

"We had sex, yeah. But werewolves are pretty fluid when it comes to the whole sexuality thing…so, maybe the three of us could—"

He stopped as Max grabbed a banana and flung it at his head. Catching it easily, Priest laughed. "You should at least consider it."

"I'll consider a threesome with a girl only if you'll consider having one with me and another guy," she countered, knowing his possessive streak would never allow it.

Priest scowled. "I was kidding, Max."

"I wasn't." She smirked. "Who knows? According to you, Dezmoon worships me. Maybe he'd jump at a chance to join the two of us in the sack."

The singular vein began to throb at the side of Priest's neck. "Very funny," he growled. Grabbing a pair of boots, he shoved his feet into them and began jerking the laces together.

Sighing, Max shook her head in disapproval. "It's such a double standard with you boys."

"Whatever," Priest said and snatched the car keys from the counter. He was clearly done with the conversation. "Let's go. We've got work to do."

Nine

"You can't still be mad. You're the one who started the whole threesome thing."

Priest had barely spoken a dozen words to Max since leaving the house. From what she could tell, they were headed to the government base positioned just north of the city. But because of traffic, that left another thirty minutes of travel with Mr. Sullen Grumpy Pants.

"I didn't pout for this long about Kuro," she continued, refusing to leave him to his moody silence. "And you two actually slept together. All Dezmoon does is stare and invade my personal space. Though he is sort of hot in an eerie, I-have-people-chained-in-the-basement-but-I-also-rescue-puppies, kind of way." Max fell silent as she pondered the thought, casually wondering if Dezmoon was into bondage.

Frowning, Priest watched her. "I know that look. Are you seriously thinking about having sex with him right now?"

"No," she answered, blushing guiltily.

"Right." His frown deepened as he looked away. "And for the record, you pouted for a solid hour about me and Kuro."

"You actually counted." Max rolled her eyes. "How old are you? Five?"

"Five and a half," he shot back, but a slow smile crept across his face.

She laughed. "Oh, that's better."

With Priest's sulk-fest broken, she switched on the radio and slouched into her seat to enjoy the rest of the ride. Slow, congested traffic coupled with the heat of the sun had always made Max drowsy, so it wasn't long before her eyelids drooped heavily with sleep…until something inexplicable happened.

Fully alert, Max sat up and tried to decipher exactly what she was feeling. The air inside the cabin had somehow been electrified—resembling the build-up just before the discharge of a static electric shock. Foreign energy surrounded her, pulling at her body like second gravity. Strange vibrations began to ripple across her skin…almost identical to what she had experienced just before the entity attacked last night. Only this feeling wasn't of some unseen creature stalking her. Rather, Max had the sense of being summoned.

"Priest," she whispered, uncertain how to explain it.

He glanced her, clearly aware something was amiss. "What's wrong?" he asked.

"I don't know." Max shook her head as if to clear it. "I think we need to get off the highway."

"Our exit is not for another five miles."

"That's not what I mean. Take the next ramp."

"Why?"

"Please, just do it."

"Okay," he said, already guiding the SUV into the far-right lane to exit. The road led to the middle of downtown, a crowded, bumper-to-bumper clusterfuck at this hour.

"Take the next left," Max said. She was following the pull, steering Priest to where it was strongest. The wisdom of that choice would be determined soon enough. "Slow down," she cautioned.

Priest was watching her with a wary, uncertain expression but obeyed her instructions. When she suddenly shouted for him to stop, he brought the SUV to an abrupt, tire-squealing halt.

"Max, what the hell?"

"It's getting weaker now. Park the car. We need to get out and walk the other way."

He unstrapped his seatbelt but made no further move. "Are you going to tell me what's going on?"

She shook her head. "I'm not sure yet. I feel something…similar to what happened last night."

His eyes grew about as big and round as saucers. "You mean when that flying thing crashed through the window and tried to rip out my liver?"

"No," Max said quickly, but after a beat of hesitation, she reconsidered. "Maybe."

"Which is it?"

Max shrugged. They were sitting there, playing twenty questions. Meanwhile, the tug was fading. "Does it matter? I thought you were programmed to never run from a fight."

Reaching for the door handle, she exited the SUV before he could utter a word of protest, but Priest moved even faster, swiftly blocking her path on the sidewalk. "You need to be sure because we can't engage with something like that in the middle of the street. We may be hard to kill, but civilians aren't."

Damn it. He was right. Searching for a clearer explanation, Max tried to better communicate what was happening. "I think this is different, Priest, but honestly, I can't be sure because I've never felt this before. My gut is telling me that I have to go and see this through, whether you're with me or not."

Priest gritted his teeth. "Okay. Fair enough," he said quietly and stepped aside.

Pausing briefly to take his hand and give it a light squeeze as thanks, Max set out at a brisk walk. She had to understand what was happening to her…and know what called to her.

They had traveled two blocks when the feeling became as strong as it had ever been.

Stopping, Max took in the surroundings and searched for anything that may have been extraordinary. Here, the pull was nearly irresistible but nothing seemed out of place. People were eating lunch inside nearby cafes, shopping within small department stores, and drinking coffee on sidewalk benches while waiting for public transportation. These humans had no idea about what sorts of creatures were living among them, stalking them, or feeding on them. They were oblivious to the formation of rifts between Earth and other far more frightening worlds. And they certainly were not aware of Max as she followed the trail of something ancient...and powerful. It was just a normal day for them.

Staring at the coffee shop across the street, Max made a closer study of the quaint little brick and mortar building, sandwiched between a rustic bicycle shop and one of those gaudy, New Age hotels featuring bold colors and abstract designs as an aesthetic lure. A few tall plants and purple daisies were potted next to the coffee shop's entrance. Coated in brazen red paint, the door stood propped open, welcoming tourists and locals alike to come enjoy the slow-roasted creations inside. Next door, a bored-looking valet manned a tiny kiosk situated in front of the hotel lobby.

Leaving the sidewalk, Max stepped into the street. Everything leading to this moment was born from an unexplained feeling. She didn't know how she knew the café was where she needed to be. She simply *knew*.

Other than blared horns from a couple of irritated drivers, Max crossed to the café without incident. Priest followed closely, stopping only to deliver a menacing glare to one driver who had dared hit the car horn twice. Immediately, the driver offered an apologetic wave and cautiously continued forward after Priest had passed.

Max had been inside this café many times before. Other than their seasonal specials, she knew the menu by heart. For most visits, a simple café au lait was enough to satisfy her bean cravings. And then there were the monstrous days where the stress of work, bills, friends, and a flatlined love life had called for the naughtier stuff—triple espresso, hazelnut syrup, topped with caramel and whipped cream. But today was different. Max hadn't come to The Toasted Bean for coffee. As it turned out, Max was just looking for a guy. She spotted him, standing next to the alleyway entrance. What was most shocking was the fact that he looked a lot like her. His complexion was dark—lighter than Max's—but still the deep bronze that olive skin gets only after hours of baking in the sun. His blond, wavy hair—almost as fair as Priest's—was trimmed neatly. And his eyes…his eyes were vertical slits where pupils should have been, surrounded by oceans of gold.

Paralyzed by awe, Max couldn't tear her gaze away from the stunning stranger whose appearance was as frightening as hers. And that he walked around boldly exposing his inhumanness—she couldn't believe it.

Between them and all around, the air hummed with energy, filling every space within the little shop. This eerie creature was the source of that power. He was also the originator of the pull currently drawing Max into his orbit. Afraid of what might happen if she were to get too close, she planted her feet and resisted. Maybe Priest sensed it too. Or maybe he just hadn't missed the way the creature scrutinized Max. Either way, he started to step forward and move into a protective position, but she stopped him. This guy may have looked like her, but for all Max knew, that was where the similarity ended. He was a total wild card.

"Don't," she whispered.

Across the room, the stranger frowned. With anger? Confusion? Max didn't know, and before she could decipher it, the energy constrained within the room seemed to shudder. Then both it and the strange man simply vanished.

Exhaling a deep breath, Max turned to Priest. "Well, that was weird. You want some coffee?"

"I think we're going to need something stronger than coffee."

"This place also has a liquor license. It's why I like it so much."

"Naturally," Priest said dryly, but followed her to the counter.

Within ten minutes, they were back inside the company SUV with steaming, whiskey-spiked coffees in hand. Priest took a long drink and set his cup aside. "Okay, I'm just going to say it." He studied her with an expression so indiscernible, Max would have had more luck translating hieroglyphics. "That guy back there looked a lot like you," he said, faltering somewhat as he spoke.

"I know," she agreed softly. Hope, confusion, and fear all warred for dominance in her heart and mind. Max simply didn't know what to feel or think. "Maybe it's time that we told my father about this." She rushed on before Priest could protest. "There's so much about where I come from that I don't know. Who I am...or what I am. I know my mother wasn't human, but I have no idea what she was. My father could tell us and maybe help us understand what we're tracking. Think about it, Priest. What if the same guy—or creature or whatever—is responsible for murdering the director, the threat to the governor, and the disappearances you were investigating before this mess started?"

Priest was shaking his head no. "We can't, Max."

"Why not?"

He turned away from her, unsuccessfully hiding the miserable expression that seized ahold of his features. "You have to trust me on this."

"Priest, I already decided last night to trust you again. Please tell me what's going on. I know you're keeping something from me—something about my father. For some reason, that's really scaring the hell out of me."

"It should," he said in a low voice and brought his gaze around to meet hers again, allowing her to see how his blue eyes brimmed with worry. "We can't tell your father, Max. Because I don't know what he'd do to you this time."

Feeling ill, she stared down at the cup clutched between her hands, ignoring the building heat that burned her fingertips through the recyclable sleeve. "He swore I'd never have to go through tests like those again."

"*Fuck*," Priest exclaimed, slamming his fist against the steering wheel.

Caught off guard, Max jerked in surprise and would have spilled coffee everywhere had he not quickly snagged the steaming beverage from her grasp. "Sorry," he said, carefully avoiding her gaze. He took far too long to situate the drink within the safe confines of a cup holder, but Max held her tongue and waited. She sensed they were on the verge of something profound. Folding both hands in his lap, Priest clenched them together. A long stretch of silence followed, and then, finally, in a tone infused with regret, he confirmed Max's deepest fears.

"Your father didn't order me to keep tabs on you this past year out of concern for your safety, Max. He's been waiting to see if new abilities will manifest since the last barrage of tests were performed. If it wasn't me, it was going to be someone else. I only took the assignment to make sure you didn't get hurt like before. If you tell your father what's happening now, he will send a team for you—and I don't know if I will be able to stop them." Gritting his teeth, Priest's voice took on a note of strain. "But I swear to you, Max. I'll die before it's me who causes you pain again."

Max wished with her whole being that she had the kind of relationship with Max Sr. where she could become indignant and vehemently dispute such slanderous accusations against her father. But she didn't. Max knew Priest's words were true even as he said them…even as betrayal chipped away a little more from her already fractured spirit. Flicking a single tear from her cheek, she strapped the seatbelt across her lap and directed her attention to the road forward.

"We'll just have to figure this out for ourselves then," she said.

*

By the time they arrived on base, Max had mostly compartmentalized the new details on her father's treachery and the role Priest played in it. How quickly the knots of forgiveness unraveled when people kept lying and creating more reasons to be hated. But right now, she couldn't process betrayal and also suitably focus on her job. So Max wisely decided to prioritize the work at hand and sort out the treachery later.

Priest walked them through several layers of security, granting Max the use of a VIP visitor's badge so she could bypass checkpoints despite not having clearance. The special badge basically gave her access to anything and everything—with the caveat of Priest's approval. Until they reached their ultimate destination, he said very little, allowing Max the space she sorely needed. But it was a double-edged sword. Though Max harbored no desire to converse with her ex-boyfriend at the moment, silence allowed her thoughts to wander to the very things she was trying to ignore. Then came the task of wrangling them back to the moment.

Of course, it had never been a secret that her father's men were under orders to watch over her, but Max thought it was because he actually cared for her well-being. She hadn't realized that her father was only waiting to drag her back to the UCC, kicking and screaming, in order to lock her in a cage again. Priest claimed he wanted to protect her from that and from her father. But Max wasn't sure how far she was willing to take her newfound trust in him—especially after his recent admission to still being in cahoots with her father. Right now, she practically had a target on her back. New abilities she didn't understand were developing, and there was a murder suspect who bore traits very similar to her own. Priest knew about all of it. He could turn her over—just like he had before. Or at least he could try to. Max's hands curled into fists at her sides. *Goddammit. I won't go without a fight.* Priest touched her shoulder, and she flinched.

"Try to relax," he said under his breath. "No one is going to lay a finger on you here. You're safe with me, Maxima. I promise."

Keeping her gaze aimed toward the floor, Max nodded by way of reply. She waited as Priest swiped his badge across a panel next to a sealed doorway and then pressed his hand into a scanner mounted beside it. Hydraulics hissed as the door was lifted, retracting toward the ceiling to allow entry. Cold air rushed upward from open floor vents, blasting Max with an eye-opening chill as she stepped into the narrow passageway.

"This is what we operators call 'The Library.' These servers contain every line of information we have on any creature that has ever crossed over. A lot of the data can be accessed remotely, but the most sensitive material is strictly confined to this room and these computers."

As if on cue, the passageway widened and a great room opened up before them. A countless number of vertical columns rose out of the floor in clusters of five. Steel plates covered three sides of each pillar, while frosted glass comprised the fourth.

Max rubbed her arms absently. "Why is it so cold in here? Are you guys afraid of the computers overheating or something?"

Priest smiled. "No."

Moving toward the nearest cluster, he gestured for her to follow. Once she reached his side, Priest wiped the frosted panel with one hand, revealing a semi-humanoid face, frozen solid in a mask of death. Max gasped.

It was probably an obvious question but one she had to ask anyway. "Is it dead?"

"This one is."

The cavernous room filled with pillars took on a new perspective. There were far more supernatural creatures coming through rifts to reach the human world than she had realized. No doubt, the rest of the USPMS was just as ignorant. It was a testament to the military that they had kept the problem so well hidden. Maybe

Director Cranke had known, but he was dead now, so little did that matter. "Are they all dead?" she asked.

Priest shook his head. "Some creatures possess abilities that could be useful to the UCC. We store those potentials here, along with whatever data we have about their species."

After a moment of hesitation, Max gingerly pressed her hand against the frosted glass. The cold was shocking. Staring at the unknown creature, it wasn't lost on her how easily it could have been her on the other side of the glass pane.

"Why did you bring me here?" she asked, her voice a whisper.

"I already told you, Max. We need to identify what attacked us. I couldn't see it, but you did. If anything like it has ever visited our world before, then there's a pretty good chance it ended up somewhere inside this room—dead or alive."

It wasn't really what Max had been asking, but she accepted his answer and decided to move on. "Okay," she said, and moved away from the glass. "Tell me what to do."

"Come on." Taking a position before a different pillar, Priest punched a sequence of keystrokes into its central controller. "I'm pulling up a catalogue of winged creatures we've encountered since the rifts first began opening. See if anything looks like what you saw last night."

Switching places with him before the pillar, Max dutifully scrolled through a long list of creatures depicted on screen, but what attacked them last night wasn't there. Working her way backward and more slowly, she double-checked just to be sure. Certain the creature was not within the Library's eerie catalogues, Max shook her head. "I don't see it."

"Damn." Sighing, Priest folded his arms across his chest, and Max's gaze was briefly drawn to his bulging biceps. "I was sure we'd find it here," he said.

She bit her lip. It was a long shot but… "Does this place have internet?"

"Yeah," he answered, but looked doubtful. "Don't say you're about to Google it, Max. Any whack job can post to the net whatever make-believe bullshit the spaceship of his or her imagination manages to beam into existence. We need fact, not fiction."

"C'mon, Priest. Stop your ranting and be a little more open-minded. All fiction is based in fact."

"Facts save lives. Fiction will get us killed."

"Just trust me," she muttered. Ignoring his objections, her fingers danced across the keys, inputting a basic description of the horror from the previous night. Reptilian head. Lion's body. Nocturnal. Carnivorous.

"Bingo," she exclaimed and tapped the screen. "That's it."

As Priest leaned closer, his eyes narrowed with suspicion. "Saurummut," he read aloud, "A part-lion, part-reptilian demon originating from the Egyptian underworld. Always female in gender, the saurummut is a soul-eater, sustained only by feeding on the hearts of its victims." He straightened. "See, that's exactly the sort of bullshit I was talking about. Max, the thing that attacked us didn't come from some mythical afterlife in Egypt."

"How can you be so sure?"

His blue eyes nearly bulged out of his head. "Because it's fucking mythology. Whether it originates from Greece, Rome, Egypt, or wherever else—that stuff is total make-believe, and I can't believe you're entertaining this."

"And I can't believe you're not," Max replied stubbornly. "Read the rest of it. The saurummut is nocturnal. Check. It can only be seen by its victims whose hearts have been torn out."

"Not check," Priest interrupted emphatically. "No one's heart got torn out and you still saw the damn thing."

"Okay, you're right about that part, but ultraviolet grenades didn't exist in ancient Egypt, so the saurummut would have been strictly invisible back then."

"*Back then*," he repeated, remaining adamant. "Rifts would have to not only be doorways to other worlds, but also to other time periods. I'm not buying it."

Turning toward him, Max exhaled a frustrated breath. She needed to get Priest on board, and to do that, she would have to switch tactics. "Let's forget about Egyptian mythology then."

"Done," he said curtly.

Frowning, Max paused and collected a few more drops of patience before continuing. "Do you believe me when I say that the creature I saw last night was half-lion, half-lizard?"

"Yes."

"It was obviously nocturnal, and the UV grenades hurt it, so it had to be photosensitive. Correct?"

"Yes and yes."

She ran her fingers down his left side, feeling the thick bandages beneath his shirt. Max didn't miss the way he shuddered slightly beneath her touch. "You do have a heart, don't you?"

"Of course," he said easily, but his brilliant eyes watched her carefully, and every part of him had tensed. The air around them was thick enough to be cut with a knife.

Max couldn't last long under his perceptive gaze before she'd be pulled under and forced to resist the urge to drag him to the floor and rip off his clothes—even while in the creepy "library." Always a stickler for the rules, no way would he have gone along with such taboo conduct. Priest was on base, and being there meant he was all business. It made what Max had to do next a lot easier.

Lightly jamming her fingers into his injured side, she made an upward raking motion like an animal might with its claws. Grunting with pain, Priest pulled away from her in a hurry. "What the fuck was that?" he said, his voice taking on a higher pitch as he gave her a bewildered look.

"I'm only proving my point. That creature—by whatever name you want to call it—was after your heart, Priest."

"You could have just said that," he grumbled, still angled away from her and guarding his ribs.

"I tried to, but you weren't listening to me."

"Well, I'm listening now. Is there anything else you would like to say without all the poking?"

"Actually, yes." She again pointed at the recessed screen within the pillar. "According to this, a saurummut does the bidding of another more powerful being. And after a saurummut consumes a heart, the victim then becomes enslaved to whomever controls the saurummut."

"I'm just going to go ahead and make the leap and land where you're aiming the crazy flag. You think the saurummut wanted to eat my heart in order for its master to be able to control me."

Max scratched her head, already beginning to second guess herself. "Okay, when you say it out loud like that, it does sound a little crazy."

"It's already been established that you're the one who is being stalked. Your boss was killed and his severed head was left on your bed. You came to my house and then some mythological creature smashed my window and trashed my guestroom trying to get to you. Common denominator in both scenarios was you, darlin'."

"I also seem to recall a certain blond-haired, blue-eyed mercenary at both scenes as well. Plus, weren't you the one investigating a series of disappearances of some high-profile citizens throughout the city? Maybe someone is after you to get you off the trail."

"Or maybe the Easter Bunny is real."

"I'm going to start poking you again."

Priest grinned in spite of her threat. "I don't know for sure if the missing people are dead, and kidnapping is a far cry from murder and dismemberment. If this is the same guy, his modus operandi has seriously changed for the worse. But," he quickly added as Max opened her mouth to protest, "I won't rule it out. Happy?"

"No, but satisfied for now."

He started to say more—something snarky Max guessed—but his cell phone vibrated inside his pocket and Priest stopped to answer it. As he checked the incoming number, his shoulders squared and he stood even taller. Max knew the call had to be from one of his superiors.

"Preesti," he answered.

She strained her ears, trying to listen in. Unfortunately, all operators within Priest's unit carried specialized phones, designed to keep information secure by dampening the soundwaves emitted from microphones. From where she stood, Max was deaf to the other side of the conversation, but the grim set of his jaw was enough to tell her it wasn't good news. Uttering a brusque "yes sir" he ended the call.

"I have to go. We just got a huge lead on those missing persons. Several teams are to report within the hour."

"Shouldn't you be happier?" she asked, testing the waters. "At least one mystery might be solved today."

Priest cut straight to the point. "I don't want to leave you, Max."

Oh. In a heartbeat of panic, she realized again they'd yet to discuss where things stood between them after last night's tryst, even without piling on the complication of Priest's most recent confession. Max swallowed and reminded herself that he, of course, was only talking pure tactics at the moment. The last thing she needed was for him to notice her getting flustered over an ambiguous turn of phrase, so she quickly deflected. "One night of crisis sex and you're already getting clingy. Go. I'll be fine. The saurummut is nocturnal, so it can't even to try to come after me for another six hours, minimum."

He frowned like he was gearing up to argue, but really, what choice did he have? Priest had orders. And with him, the job always came first—no matter what. "Okay," he eventually relented. "But tell me where you're going, so Kuro can meet you. And promise me that you won't leave her side."

"Since it's Sunday and supposed to be my day off, I think I'll go to Gents & Belles for a drink or two…check in with my former roommates."

"That's good. Tell Arabella I said hello."

"I will. Is my apartment still off limits or have your people cleared it?"

"It's off limits."

"Ugh. It's laundry day, Priest. I have no clothes and I need to finish the kapre report by tomorrow. Can't you call someone, so I can get in there? And how did your place get cleared so fast and mine is still a red zone?"

"Borrow some clean clothes from Arabella. Come back to my place later to work on the report. I'm a senior officer, so there are some perks, but no, I can't get your apartment cleared any sooner." Pulling her close, he gently kissed her forehead, mostly dispelling her petulant mood. "Max, I want you to stay at my townhouse until this is over."

Quite capable of recognizing a futile argument when it came to Priest, Max sometimes ignored good sense and started one anyway. This, however, was not one of those times. What she needed was some space between them, so she could think. "Fine," she said, trying not to appear to agree too quickly.

Taking her hand, he ushered her out of the library and across the base at a hurried pace, pausing only to bark a few orders to straggling members of his unit. Once they'd reached the parking lot, Priest passed her a set of keys to the SUV. "Your car is still at your agency, so use mine. Go straight to Gents & Belles. Kuro will already be there."

"I will," she promised as she climbed up into the tan leather driver's seat.

"Max," he called, catching the door before she could close it.

"Yeah?" she prodded softly when he didn't say anything.

"It wasn't crisis sex," he finally said, drilling her with those radioactive eyes—full of something Max was afraid to name, something that would only drag her deeper into a minefield of imminent hurt. "At least to me it wasn't."

A fist-sized knot lodged within her airway, forcing Max to clear her throat just to breathe. "Okay," she answered noncommittally. If the past twenty-four hours had taught her anything, it was that she could never really be quite certain of where she stood with Priest. "Good hunting out there."

Ten

When Max arrived at Gents & Belles, Arabella was on stage, performing a sultry, two-song routine, so Max found a spot to wait for the grand finale. Jensen was tending bar and slid a Manhattan in front Max just as she sat down. He must have spotted her soon after she walked in.

Max grabbed the drink as if it were a lifeline, uttered a quick thank you, and took a long swallow.

Jensen made a sympathetic noise. "Rough day?"

"Rough three days," Max amended.

Even in the dim lighting, she saw how his almond-shaped, hazel eyes took on a mischievous glint. "Does it have anything to do with Priest coming back around?"

Max nearly slammed the drink down. Scrubbing her face with both hands, she wheezed out a frustrated breath. "Jeez. Does everyone know about that?"

"Max, it's me."

Jensen Tanaka was probably just as beautiful as Arabella, but in his own way. The simple red t-shirt he wore hugged his chest and biceps in the just the right manner, showcasing a sculpted dancer's body beneath the cotton-blend material. It probably wasn't by accident that the color of his shirt also matched the streaks in his perfectly styled, longish, jet black hair. As far as Max knew, he was fully human, and advanced genetics weren't responsible for his good looks. With his mixed heritage, Jensen had simply lucked out in getting the best features from both gene pools. Great cheek bones, awesome hair, and a skin tone that never needed tanning—to name a few.

Jensen leaned across the counter. "And did you really think Arabella was going to keep such a golden little nugget about you and Priest to herself, especially when she needs me to cover her waitressing shift so she can go on a date tonight?"

"Arabella bartered information on my personal affairs in exchange for a favor? Wow." Max pressed the cool glass to her lips and nursed another generous swig, letting the sweet, smoky liquid warm the back of her throat. "But that means you have to work a double then—dayshift bartender and wait staff tonight. That's going to be rough. I didn't realize news about my disastrous love life held so much value to you."

Straightening, Jensen pressed his lips together in a thin line of annoyance. His expression gradually smoothed as he began polishing the bar with a towel. Reaching underneath the counter, he grabbed two glasses, set them in front of Max, and filled both with double shots of tequila. "You know I'm a gossip," he said, and winked. "It's a by-product of this toxic environment." He held up his glass and tapped it lightly against hers. "Cheers."

"Cheers," she echoed and threw back the shot, wincing as the liquor burned a trail all the way down to her belly. Max preferred bourbon. Its sweetness was much easier on the palate.

"Besides," he said, pouring a second round. "It pays to know if the big, bad, platinum commando is still available. Some of these girls would drive a spiked heel into a bitch's back to get the tiniest bit of insight on Priest."

Max just about fell off the bar stool. Even when they were together, Gents & Belles' fluid, almost-anything-goes atmosphere had never really been Priest's sort of scene. His boot strings were laced far too straight. "He's been coming around here?"

"Yeah, but he seemed more interested in the crowd than in the dancers. I think he might have been working. Which is odd because I didn't think Priest did security."

Thinking back to the gala, she murmured, "I used to think so too." Then she downed the second glass of tequila and tipped the low ball to her lips, drinking until the Manhattan was drained.

Jensen's eyes widened as he gave a slight chuckle. "Whoa. Slow down. You know you're a mean drunk, Max."

"Am not." She nudged the glass toward him— a big hint regarding her desire for a refill. "And I'm not even buzzed yet, princess."

Raising both eyebrows, Jensen swapped the used glass for a clean one and promptly mixed another Manhattan, but as she reached for it, Arabella slid into the chair next to her and plucked the drink right out of Max's grasp. Arabella's lengthy, reddish locks were made even longer and fuller by temporary extensions, creating a cascade of envy-inducing tresses. Besides stiletto heels and a pleated skirt short enough to expose her ass cheeks, she wore nothing else, leaving her perky, 30F breasts and pink nipples on full, traffic-stopping display. Max had visited the club so many times, she barely batted an eyelash at its full-scale nudity— even when it came to her best friend.

"How'd you like the finale?" Arabella asked after helping herself to the drink intended for Max.

"The upside down split and twist?"

"Followed by the slow back-flip, pole walk-off."

Nodding, Max laughed. "It was incredible. I'd throw a hundred dollars at you."

Happy with the praise, Arabella grinned and surrendered the remainder of the Manhattan. Meanwhile, Jensen chimed in with his two cents. "Max, you don't have a hundred dollars. And Arabella, you wasted those moves on non-existent clientele. It rarely gets any deader in here."

Even as her smile faded, Arabella lifted her chin a bit higher. "Must you always be the cynic?"

"Someone has to keep you humble."

"Well, negativity isn't attractive on anyone."

Max took another swallow of bourbon, watching the two of them spar over the rim of her glass. The sexual tension between Arabella and Jensen always made for fascinating entertainment. Though they'd never dated, Max knew for a fact that they had slept together on at least one drunken occasion.

"I'm not being negative. I'm stating facts," Jensen insisted.

Arabella's spine pulled a little straighter and her smile returned, though it didn't quite reach her eyes. "It wasn't a waste. It was practice." She looked pointedly at Max, seeking backup.

"Don't let Jensen get that sparkly thong of yours in a wad," Max counseled. "You were great out there, and I'm sure you'll be even better when the club is packed out. However…" Max paused to take another sip of her drink while Arabella and Jensen waited for her to conclude her role as mediator. "I really do only have seventy-three dollars in my bank account," she finished with a shrug.

The comment won a small laugh from them both. "I guess this afternoon's tab must be on the house then," Jensen said as he poured more tequila. He slid the second glass to Arabella. "Bottoms up, Ari. Pre-game for your hot date tonight."

"Gladly," she said and started to bring the shot to her lips, but Max stopped her.

"Seven years of bad sex unless you look me in the eyes before taking that."

"Damn, I forgot."

Earnestly meeting Arabella's gaze, Max struggled to match her best friend's intensity without bursting into a fit of giggles. Between the alcoholic coffee several hours earlier, two Manhattans, and six—now nine—ounces of tequila, maybe she had actually gotten a little tipsy.

"If you two were to kiss right now, my life would be complete."

"Dream on," Max said, rolling her eyes.

"Hey," Arabella protested with a hot-pink pout. "You wouldn't kiss me?"

"If you weren't topless at the moment, sure, why not," Max replied in a placating tone.

"Yes!" Jensen exclaimed from behind the bar. "Ari, cover up those jugs. I'll give you the shirt off my back."

"Stop talking, Jensen." The look Arabella leveled at him was near feral, making Max think of a certain other woman possessing wolf-like characteristics. She cringed. Max had been so preoccupied with trying to ~~process~~ drink away the craziness that had transpired over the past two days and Priest's huge, cherry topper admission about her father that she had completely forgotten about Kuro.

"Shit," she muttered. It'd be something else for Priest to give her grief about later.

Arabella raised an eyebrow. "What's up?"

"I was supposed to meet someone here, and I forgot."

"Don't worry. She's still here," Jensen said.

"What?" Max's head jerked up in surprise. "How do you know that?"

He nodded toward the far left of the stage, indicating a dark corner beneath the dim blue lights. "I've never seen her in here before, but she's been watching you since you walked in. She's kind of got this kind of sexy, homeless meth-head thing going on."

Arabella blinked at him. "I am literally beginning to think that you would fuck anything."

"Kittens," Jensen deadpanned. "I don't fuck kittens."

Arabella ignored the comment, searching instead for Max's newest companion. "She is kind of cute. Friend of yours, Max?"

"Not exactly." Max sighed. "So much has happened since I last saw you, Ari. Someone broke into my apartment. Priest and I were attacked at his home, and my boss was murdered."

As Max spoke, Arabella and Jensen's expressions evolved with increasing shock. Max didn't blame them. "I also found out that Priest was under orders from my father to watch me this entire time. If any new abilities manifested, I was to be taken back to the labs for testing."

"What the hell?" Arabella exclaimed exactly as Jensen pounded the bar top and growled, *"That sonofabitch."*

Max winced. "It's a lot to take in." She'd purposefully left out the revelations about Kevin the wendigo and how Cranke's head was left as a bloody deposit on her queen-sized bed.

Partial nudity aside, Arabella pulled Max close, embracing her in a long, sympathetic hug. As Max hugged her back, she glanced at Jensen over Arabella's shoulder, expecting him to say something pervy, but he surprised her. One look at Jensen, and it was obvious that he was in no mood to tell lewd jokes. His hands were balled into white-knuckled fists, trembling as they rested atop the counter. Red splotches marred the skin around his neck and ears. Even his hazel-colored eyes seemed to have taken on a sort of rust-like hue. Basically, he looked about as angry as Max had ever seen him.

Arabella noticed too. "You okay?" she asked, releasing Max.

Jensen gritted his teeth. "I swear if he tries to come for you again, I will kill him."

Arabella scoffed at the threat. "Priest would rip out your spine and strangle you with it. But you'd be sweet for trying." She finished with a smile sugary enough to soften the insult to Jensen's virility.

It's okay." Max reached for Jensen's hand, trying to get him to relax. "Priest is not on my father's side in this." Mentally crossing her fingers, she armored her heart and added, "I think we can trust him."

Jensen shook his head. "Priest is dangerous. The only reason he wasn't put down with the rest of that psycho unit was because he wasn't like the others. The UCC saw something in Priest that they wanted, so they found a way to implant inhibitors in his freaking brain."

Shocked, Max pulled away. The limited information she knew about Priest's origins was obtained on a strictly need-to-know basis and only because she was an employee of the UCC. Priest had revealed some secrets during the course of their failed relationship, but nothing like what Jensen described. "How could you possibly know that?"

"It doesn't matter. What you need to understand is that Priest doesn't have the final say in what he does. The UCC controls him. If Priest is ordered to bring you in, he will do it. You need to get as far away from him as you can."

Jensen's angry stare drilled into Max, hammering home his message. Conveniently, a couple sat down at the other end of the bar, and without a word, Jensen left to serve them. Max watched him walk away, inert with her feelings of bewilderment. Jensen was one of her closest friends and had no reason to lie to her, yet the incredible story he'd just told was enough to give anyone pause.

Arabella whistled, breaking Max's thought trance. "Wow. His feathers sure got pretty ruffled. Even my slovenly housekeeping has never pissed him off like that."

"He and Priest were never the best of friends." Max chewed her lip worriedly. "Do you think what he said was true?"

Arabella shrugged. "Who knows? I wouldn't put anything past the UCC. The better question is, do you believe it?"

"I honestly don't know." Max blew out a soft breath. "For now, I'll just file it under 'deal with later.'"

"Good idea." Arabella twirled around on the stool. "Enough about that. I'm heartbroken because I never got to peel him out of that suit, but Cranke was sort of a friend to you, right? I only met the guy once and I still can't believe he's gone. How are you dealing with everything? And your apartment, is it safe? Come stay with me for a few days. Or better yet, just move back in."

"Let's not go overboard," Max said waving her hands in protest. "Thanks for the offer, but I'm okay, Ari. My apartment, however, is not…which brings me to another important subject. But before we talk about it, you have to swear not to tell Jensen."

Arabella frowned. "Why? We pretty much tell him everything."

"I know," Max said, feeling guilty for even asking. "But considering how he just reacted…"

"Oh," Arabella said, understanding immediately. "This is about Priest."

"Yeah," Max admitted but stopped, stalling for a few more seconds of time when Arabella didn't know the truth.

"Spit it out," Arabella urged, now literally perched at the edge of her seat.

"We had sex," Max blurted out.

Arabella gasped. "Real penis-pounding-your-vagina sex?"

"Yes."

"When?"

"Last night." Max glanced away. "Several times."

"Oh.My.God."

"Yeah."

"Ohmygod, Max."

Max covered her face with her hands. "I know."

Arabella's laughter came as a surprise, causing Max to look up. "I knew it," her friend said. "And you better not be having second thoughts about it because you're never getting rid of him now."

Antsy for the other shoe to drop, Max glanced at Kuro, aware too late that the she-wolf may have been capable of overhearing the entire conversation. Hopefully, the music was loud enough to prevent even supernatural eavesdropping. "You're not mad?"

"Hell no." Arabella lost her self-satisfied smirk long enough to look confused. "Unless it wasn't good. He hasn't lost the ability to make you explode a thousand times has he?"

Max blushed as her mind strayed to the previous night. "His skills are still very much intact."

"Well then no, I'm not mad. If you're happy, I'm happy. Priest isn't the worst you could do."

"Gee thanks."

"Anytime." Arabella glanced at the clock behind the bar. "I've got to go soon. Can't have my first date with hot café manager in this get up. But first, tell me what does the warrior sprite have to do with the hellacious time you've been having?"

"Her name is Kuro, and she works with Priest. He was called away to lead his team on mission, so he sent Kuro to watch my back until he returns."

Arabella considered the she-wolf with knitted eyebrows. "What? Is she going to protect you from the other woodland fairies? Maybe I should cancel my date." Arabella cracked her knuckles. "It's been awhile since I got to hit someone."

"No, Arabella. I can't put you in that kind of danger." *Shit*, Max reprimanded herself mentally. Had she said too much? "Besides, Kuru is a werewolf. She's a lot more dangerous than she looks."

Arabella still appeared skeptical. Anyone whose DNA skirted the normal human make-up knew how rare a true werewolf was, and for one to be working with the government—well, that was unheard of. Max could tell Arabella wanted to ask more questions, but to her relief, she only nodded instead. "Okay. But call me tonight. I mean it. Even if my fat ass is bent over a couch and on the receiving end of something magical, I'll answer."

"Firstly, there's nothing fat about your ass. And secondly, I really hope you wouldn't answer the phone in the middle of something like that."

"Max, promise you'll call me."

"Okay. I promise."

Satisfied, Arabella slid off the bar stool, flashing a pair of perfect ass cheeks as she sashayed to the locker rooms.

*

Jensen continued to avoid Max even after Arabella left, so Max put down as much of a tip as she could afford and exited the club. Since Kuro wasn't exactly big on small talk, there had been no real reason to approach the she-wolf inside. As Max crossed the parking lot in the fading afternoon light, she thought about everything Jensen had said, still wondering how he knew what he knew, and also struggling to decide if she should believe it. A nagging feeling pulled at her gut—as if her subconscious wanted her to remember something important—but she couldn't quite grasp what it was.

Gents & Belles regular clientele usually arrived with the setting sun, and this evening was no different, so there were quite a few more cars in the lot than when Max had initially arrived. However, there weren't so many that she couldn't instantly notice the two identical SUVs parked side by side as she rounded the corner. One of the vehicles—the one issued to Priest— was what she'd driven. The sight of the other made Max freeze in her tracks. Whoever had parked there obviously knew she was in the club and had little interest in concealing their presence. Either they were a friend or a very confident foe. Lifting her shirttail, Max rested one hand on the cool steel of the revolver at her hip. Until she had an answer, she was going to take every precaution.

Approaching the vehicles slowly, Max alternated between checking her surroundings and looking for signs of anyone being in the second SUV. If no one was inside, then they were out here, watching her. Unfortunately, the military-issued cars had windows covered in tint dark enough to render visibility from the outside to damn near zero.

Max may have not had a supernatural sense of smell, but her hearing was five times better than any human's, so when the faintest rustle of fabric reached her ears, she spun around, depressing the spring-loaded release with her thumb, but was careful to keep her finger free of the trigger until the revolver was aimed point-blank at the asshole who was trying to sneak up on her.

"One of these days," a graveled voiced called out, "Priest should teach you how to stay downwind."

Lowering the revolver, Max threw back her head and suppressed a groan. *Fucking Dutch.* Carter "Dutch" Lasseter was probably the last person she wanted to deal with at the moment. "What are you doing here?"

"That's a good question," he answered deliberately, accentuating his natural southern drawl. He rubbed his ear, assessing Max with an unblinking appraisal. "Priest ordered me out here, but he was pretty tight-lipped about the why part." A strange smile seemed to twitch involuntarily across his lips, as if the expression were trying to possess them. "I would love to know what it is that is so special about you. Something tells me it's not just because you're the colonel's daughter."

Squinting, Dutch made a step toward Max, and she reflexively took one back to equalize the distance between them. It wasn't that Max was

198

afraid of him. Though calling Priest and Dutch friends would have a been a serious stretch to describe their relationship, Max had no reason to believe Dutch would ever hurt her—mainly because he seemed loyal to Priest. Yet, for no definable reason, the creepy-crawly feeling Max got whenever Dutch came around, touched her on a cellular level.

Whereas Priest was team leader, Dutch was second in command of a six-member unit of operators. That fact alone made it increasingly odd for Dutch to be there instead of with Priest on a high-stakes hunt. And even odder was remembering Priest's assurance that none of his men would be involved in her precautionary guardianship.

A product of Project Washington, Dutch—like Priest—was an artificially engineered lifeform who had been spared from extinction. But unlike Priest, Dutch wasn't considered stable enough to lead his own unit. Over the years, Max had endured several encounters with the soldier. Each time, after about five minutes of exposure, Max could literally feel her skin begin to crawl, trying in vain to retreat from Dutch's strange energy. Since he and Priest were comrades—and Priest trusted the fellow operator with his life—Max did her best to give Dutch the benefit of the doubt but also remain vigilant. Doing so was incredibly difficult at times like this when he was shifting between periods of somewhat balanced normalcy and an inhuman, almost predacious demeanor.

Blond-haired and blue-eyed like Priest, Dutch's locks were longer and darker. His eyes were harsher and of a deeper blue—like an angry sea—made to stand out even more by the thick beard that covered his jaw.

When Dutch made a second, sort of halting move toward her, Max once again stepped out of reach.

"I don't bite, Max." And then as if to be contrary to that very pledge, Dutch flashed his teeth in an ambiguous smile. "At least not until you ask me to."

Before Max could answer, Kuro—out of nowhere—appeared behind Dutch. Her expression was bored, but her tone was icy enough to freeze the pavement beneath their feet. "Touch her and if I don't manage to kill you, Priest sure as hell will."

Dutch's shoulders stiffened as his overly-confident posturing faltered. "Kuro," he drawled without turning to face the she-wolf. "I thought Priest kept you on a much shorter leash."

Kuro smirked, unaffected by the insult. "I'm only stretching my legs." Her wild gaze shifted to Max. "You okay?"

"Yeah. Dutch is just being his usual, charming self."

"That explains why you drew your gun."

Max flinched. Looking down, she once more became aware of the heavy steel clutched within her hand. "A girl can never be too careful," she said mildly and holstered the weapon in one swift maneuver.

Dutch adopted an injured look. "You ladies act like I'm some kind of miscreant."

"No," Max said. "You're just unpredictable." Turning away from the both of them, Max walked to Priest's SUV with resolute strides. "Stay away from me, Dutch. One babysitter is enough."

"I won't make any promises," he called softly just as she closed the driver's side door.

With a tangible barrier between her and Dutch's strange energy, Max relaxed behind the steering wheel. Mental instability aside, Dutch was one of the UCC's most capable operators. And he was definitely the most dangerous of the unit Priest commanded. If Priest had seen fit to send that guy to look after her, he must have been even more worried about her safety than he'd previously let on. But if Priest hadn't sent him...well that would be pretty fucking problematic.

Eleven

Halfway through the kapre report part deux and on her third glass of Bordeaux, Max set the laptop aside and went to Priest's bedroom window. Crooking one finger into the blinds, she cracked them open enough to peek outside. The black SUV was still parked across the street. No doubt it was Dutch. The eerie henchman had ignored Max's request for him to stay away and followed her from Gents & Belles, parking at the townhouse just before dusk. At least Kuro had the decency to remain at a distance and keep out of sight while fulfilling her duties as bodyguard, even if it stemmed from the she-wolf's own instinct to be a solitary creature.

Breathing a sigh, Max left the window and flopped onto the bed. She had yet to hear from Priest and had no idea if he would be coming home tonight or not. Maybe having a moody werewolf and a deranged super soldier watching her six wasn't such a bad thing. It was nightfall, which meant—were the internet actually correct—the saurummut was free to roam. The soul eater could come for Max if its master wished it. But what if Priest was who the saurummut truly wanted?

Shaking her head, Max took another sip of wine. She wasn't going to worry about that. Priest was surrounded by capable fighters who had brought down creatures much bigger and deadlier than a flying, demon hybrid. If the saurummut wanted Priest's heart, it was going to have a helluva fight on its hands. The same held true if it wanted hers.

Before returning to the townhouse, Max had gone by the agency and retrieved the duffel from the trunk of her car. Between her ammo bag and Priest's closet armory, she had enough firepower to take down an army of saurummuts—as long as she found a way to aim in the right direction. Ultraviolent grenades would help with that. Unfortunately, only two of the specialized explosives remained in Priest's stash. Such a short supply was motivation to make the first one count.

Despite the late hour, Max was still fully dressed—boots and all. She wasn't about to be surprised with her pants down. However prepared, nothing changed the fact that waiting sucked. Max drummed her fingers against the mattress. She sorely needed some distraction other than finishing that damned report, but couldn't risk turning on the television. Dividing her attention could have meant realizing ten seconds slower that the saurummut was upon her. An unacceptable risk.

Dozens of books lined the shelves of three built-in, floor-to-ceiling bookshelves situated within Priest's bedroom, and reading one of them would have succeeded in taking her mind off the night ahead, but Max had never been much of a reader. Literature was more Priest's thing. So, accepting her limited options, she drained the last of the wine, retrieved the laptop, and tackled page four, delivering her best assessment of the kapre's advanced camouflage. As she typed, Max began to consider things she hadn't while compiling the maiden version of the kapre report. Maybe it was because of Priest's unsettling admission or his cautionary urgings about her father. Whatever the cause, Max began having second thoughts. No doubt every word of her report would be forwarded to the UCC, where they would certainly drool over the potential military application of being able to genetically harness invisible camouflage. The Paranormal Marshal Services only issued bounties for fugitives, but Unified Combatant Command was held to no such restrictions. A strike force could be sent after any target deemed worthy of government interest. The thought caused Max's fingers to pause on the keyboard. This discovery definitely had the potential to make tree giants of special interest to the UCC.

Shit.

After a mental war of morality, Max highlighted the last four paragraphs and hit delete. Tree giants were peaceful creatures, and Nihilson had been too, until contracting rabies.

She couldn't put his entire species at the mercy of coalition forces. It wouldn't be right. But now it was two huge things she had to lie about. Between omitting Kalista's role in Nihilson's termination and making no mention of the kapre's ability to render itself invisible, Max's report had officially become more fiction than fact. On the bright side, the story at least seemed more credulous that she could defeat a kapre without backup.

Half an hour later, Max was satisfied with the completed, somewhat truthful account of Friday night's takedown. After hitting print, she stood up and stretched. It was past midnight. Dutch continued to lurk outside, Kuro undoubtedly roamed close by, but still no word from Priest. Max was getting tired, yet sleep was out of the question.

Empty wine bottle in tow, she made her way downstairs to the kitchen and put on a pot of coffee, brewing it extra black for the concentrated dose of caffeine. She browsed through a stack of mail left on the counter, amused to discover the latest issues of *Gourmet Home* and *Bass Strings*. How a monthly magazine written exclusively about guitars could ever be interesting was beyond any stretch of Max's imagination, so she picked up the issue of *Gourmet Home* and idly thumbed through about twenty pages of recipes before the coffee maker chimed to indicate a completed brew. Tossing the magazine aside, Max grabbed the carafe and intended to fill a large, mug but stopped when sudden, inexplicable pain rammed into her skull with the force of a double-decker bus. Some part of her brain registered the sound of shattering glass as the carafe struck the tiled floor and broke into a thousand pieces. But then Max was transported to another place—another time—and Priest's kitchen no longer existed.

Max stared down at her fingers, now buried in dark, pebbly soil where massive pine trees grew all around, surrounding her. Things were shifting in and out of focus because the pain…the pain was excruciating. Gritting her teeth, Max pushed to her knees and then climbed to her feet. Unless she'd developed the magical ability of teleportation within the last few minutes, what she was seeing couldn't be real. And yet, there she stood in a dense forest, breathing the crisp night air and watching thick, white clouds stretch across a navy-blue sky, partially blocking the moon's light from reaching the woodland below and casting shadows throughout its acreage.

A horrible sense of dread burrowed into Max's stomach. It, along with the throbbing ache in her skull, left her wanting to vomit. Something was wrong. Terribly wrong. She knew that finding out what would change her life forever.

Biting back a sob, Max lurched forward as her feet moved with their own volition, carrying her toward the awful thing. She didn't want to see it. She didn't want to go, but she had to. She had to face what was happening—what had happened.

And then Max heard it. A plea. A whisper. Her name said so softly, she should never have been able to hear it.

The atmosphere changed, growing so cold Max could barely stand it. The sky began to change too, morphing into brilliant hues of golden sapphires, replacing the moon with orange fire that swirled and rippled through the darkness. The feeling in her gut intensified. What lay beyond the incredible lights was the source of her dread.

Hearing her name once more, Max's blood turned to ice. Moving stiffly, she turned to face the sound. "No," she croaked, wanting to crumble to the ground. "Priest, no."

He was dressed in full tactical gear. Wherever his skin showed was layered with drying, crusted blood. More blood matted his hair and streaked his face. His eyes were all wrong, dull and cloudy as if enshrouded in thin, white veils. Instead of walking toward her, his entire body shimmered out of focus, slowly disappearing only to reappear suddenly and right next to her. Max wasn't afraid. It was Priest. She could never fear him in any form.

He touched her face, watching her with a wretched, haunting smile. "You're too late," he said softly. "Goodbye, Max."

"I don't understand," she whispered. "What are you trying to tell me?"

His bloodied fingers rubbed her cheek. "You're going to be okay."

Max frowned. Everything about him felt real. The way he caressed her skin. The smell of blood on his hands. Even the sweat stains from an adrenaline-fueled battle. But this wasn't Priest. It was a phantom. A product of her imagination—or mental illness.

No. Max closed her eyes and reopened them. There had to be a reason why this phantom kept appearing to her. Was Priest in trouble?

Grabbing his hand—it was so cold, too cold—Max squeezed. "Priest, where are you right now?"

The phantom only shook his head, still wearing that expression of utter loss.

In his silence, her answer came from an unexpected source. "Oh, you are but a fledging, aren't you?"

Max spun around. Startled by the revelation of who had spoken, she stumbled backward, falling into the phantom Priest. Luckily, he was as solid as the real thing.

"Dear sister," the man continued speaking as his golden eyes narrowed in amusement at her obvious duress. "Your beloved will die tonight, unless you save him."

Max stared, speechless and not quite able to believe what she was seeing. The creature was identical to the one who had summoned her to the coffee shop. And more notably, he looked a lot like Max. Though his hair was blonder and both eyes were marked by vertical slits.

"Yes. I am the one who visited you before," he said as if reading her thoughts. The air began to vibrate, humming with threads of energy so thick Max could have played them like guitar strings. "You have many questions, but there isn't time."

The vibrations increased and the tendrils of power began to pull Max toward the strange man. This time, she did not resist. Staring into his unearthly gaze, she found recognition. And that was terrifying.

The man touched her hand, and a trail of golden light blazed beneath his fingers. "Save your beloved. Go to him now."

That uncanny stare held Max, pulling her under like quicksand. Her heart pounded. She didn't know what to think, what to believe.

A sudden pulse erupted as a massive outpouring of energy radiated from the creature. Then the forest was gone and Max was once again in Priest's kitchen, leaning against the counter, trembling and gasping to regain her breath.

Collecting her wits enough to move, Max took a valium to settle her nerves and sank to the bathroom floor until she could be certain the reality she saw was her own. As she fought for clarity, several other dilemmas unraveled within her mind.

Max ultimately concluded that the creature—the man who looked like her—wasn't there to harm her. At least not yet. Something about him was certainly frightening—but not his looks. Every day, Max saw too similar a face in the mirror.

More pressingly, Max no longer believed it was Priest who had sent Dutch. The soldier was there at her father's behest. She couldn't be one hundred percent certain—she had no evidence—but her gut knew it was the more logical scenario. Her father's interest in keeping tabs on his daughter's burgeoning abilities had obviously supplanted the need for one of command's best soldiers to assist in the hunt for an incredibly dangerous adversary. And now, because of her father, if Max were to relinquish her hold on reality and believe a vision (one that simply could have been an extremely unhealthy manifestation of her imagination…or a relapse into psychosis), Priest was going to die.

Decision made, Max stood up and left the bathroom. Retrieving her duffle, she secured the bag across her shoulder, opened a second story window, and stepped from the ledge. She didn't have time for stairwells or doors. What she was about to do was ballsy, illegal, and would draw the ire of her father—maybe even cause him to lock her up again. But Max was beyond that. Priest needed her. And if it turned out that she was being a crazy person, taking the wrong dosage of pills, and Priest didn't actually need her—well then, nothing had really changed.

Dutch, of course, saw her coming and started to intercept, but three armor-piercing rounds fired into the SUV door and side paneling bought Max enough time to beat him to the pavement. Driving her boot into the door, she put all her weight behind it, slamming the door shut again. With two quick, successive chops of the tomahawk, she smashed the window. Thrusting the blunted edge forward, she hit Dutch in the head hard enough to stun him, but not cause serious or permanent damage. Hopefully.

Reaching inside the SUV, Max locked the door and ripped off the handle. If Dutch wanted to get out, he'd have to use a different exit, and Max was pretty confident she could shoot him first.

Touching his temple, Dutch looked incredulously at the blood on his fingertips and

211

then again at Max. He growled. "What the fuck do you think you're doing?"

Her stomach churned nervously. Max really hoped she had guessed right. "I know Priest didn't send you here."

"So what?" Dutch's stare got even wider. "You shoot my truck and bash in my fucking skull?"

"I need to know where he is."

"Your father or Priest?"

Max swallowed. "Priest."

"Well both locations are classified, sweetcheeks."

Without thinking, Max hit him again with the Shrike. It was a light jab and made with the blunt end, but was enough to make the super soldier's nose bleed. *"Fuck,"* Dutch said, dragging out the word in two pained but livid syllables.

Max winced. She'd probably fractured his nasal bone. "I'm sorry, Dutch. But I really don't have time for this. Tell me where he is."

"You are fucking nuts," he muttered under his breath. When he reached for the glove compartment, Max whipped the revolver up and held it right next to his cheek. He stopped mid-movement. "Take it easy. I'm going to give you what you need to track him."

Max kept silent. The fifty caliber bullets loaded in her revolver would obliterate the very bones in Dutch's head, and he knew that. So Max let him decide whether or not to risk reaching for anything other than a GPS tracker.

Wisely, Dutch cooperated. He procured a small, rectangular object about the size of the cell phone from the compartment. It was similar to what Priest had used to follow Kuro to Max's apartment. "All operators have implants now," Dutch explained, still sounding pissed as he keyed a code into the device. The screen lit up and he entered a second sequence of numbers. A small red dot began blinking on the display. "That's your guy," he said and offered the tracker to Max. "Head north. It looks like he's about an hour from here."

Securing the tomahawk between her shoulder blades, she took the device but was careful to keep her eyes trained on Dutch and the revolver steady on his face. "Thank you," she said, already backing away and hoping she'd remembered to grab the damn car keys.

Then a voice spoke directly next to Max's ear, surprising her enough to almost cause her to pull the trigger. Both she and Dutch swore at the same time.

Indifferent to the fact that she had quite nearly caused the end of Dutch's existence—or at least a lifelong maiming—Kuro crossed her arms. "What's going on, Max?"

Max shook her head. *Damn, that wolf can move quietly.* "Priest is in trouble, Kuro. Please don't try to stop me."

The she-wolf narrowed her eyes. "In trouble how?"

"I don't know exactly."

"Then how do you know he's in trouble?"

Max bit her lip. "I can't say." *Especially not in front of one of my father's minions.* "But I have to go. I know this puts you in a bad position, and I'm sorry for that."

After a tense moment, Kuro shrugged. "I actually wish I could help you, but I can't be near Priest's operation. Command will know. And they have my family."

Max nodded. "It's okay. I understand." She started to keep moving, but Kuro spoke again, stopping her.

"I will make sure he doesn't follow you."

Max hesitated, frowning. She didn't want anything bad to happen to Kuro's pups on her account. "Won't that cause trouble for you?"

The she-wolf bared her teeth and then snapped them together. "Dutch may be an asshole, but he's no snitch."

Twelve

It took several attempts, plus coming within a hair of rolling Priest's SUV—twice—before Max found the switch to activate the emergency license plate, signaling to any law enforcement that the vehicle was military-issued, in the middle of something important, and not to messed with. Max was free to speed and make kamikaze maneuvers as necessary without worry of interference.

Still, she only managed to shave seventeen minutes off of the estimated ETA, and by the time she steered the SUV off-road and covered five miles on a steep, mountainous service road, the red dot had stopped moving.

Heart in throat, Max continued as far as the road would take her, before putting the gearshift in park and exiting the SUV to step into darkness. She looked down at the GPS for guidance, but the little device trembled in her hand, distorting the onscreen image. Taking a deep breath, Max closed her eyes. *Get your shit together,* she said silently. Then she squared her shoulders and headed north.

Despite carrying a small arsenal and surplus ammo, it was an unavoidable fact that Max was alone, without backup, heading toward an unknown danger. Hunting a paranormal escapee was different. Before undertaking any sort of marshal-related chase, Max received a complete profile of the fugitive creature and knew exactly what species she was after, as well as any special abilities or weaknesses. This pursuit came with no such luxury. Max was blind and likely unprepared for whatever she was about to face. However, she couldn't let that stop her—not if Priest needed help.

Picking her way through darkness, Max navigated to the red dot's stagnant position, doing her best to remain as quiet as possible. Every step brought her closer to Priest, and every step intensified the knots balled within her stomach. She had almost reached the targeted coordinates when she heard it.

Snap.

A twig had splintered from less than ten feet away. Cursing silently, Max tucked the tracker into her belt and used her ears to search the forest. If her nerves had been composed of more pliant stuff, she probably would have lost it on realizing that what had broken the twig actually stood right next to her. Instead, she stepped away while simultaneously bringing the revolver up and around to fire one carefully aimed shot. The gun exploded, and Max glimpsed a flurry of movement before her hand was knocked sideways, sending the bullet blasting through the trunk of a nearby tree. Aided by the light of the muzzle flash, she saw who had been fast enough to execute such a daring maneuver.

A startled sound of anger, joy, and relief escaped Max's lips as she holstered her weapon and threw her arms around Priest's neck. "I was so worried," she said, burying her face against his chest. "What happened? Are you hurt?"

A few seconds lapsed before Priest returned the embrace. He was oddly silent, considering Max had ditched her bodyguard and rushed into the middle of an active operation. Still hugging him, Max figured Priest was deciding how much to yell at her, but then the nervous feeling returned to her belly and doubt set in.

Maybe something else is wrong.

Backing away, she looked Priest over as he stared back at her, unnaturally still and studying her with equal intensity.

Max licked her lips, noticing for the first time a strange, sulfuric smell in the surrounding air. "Are you hurt?" she repeated.

Finally, he moved, slowly shaking his head from side to side.

Other than an unshakeable feeling that something huge was amiss, Max wasn't entirely sure why but she eased one hand toward her hip, seeking the cold reassurance of steel. Even in darkness, she saw the change, the moment when

Priest became something far less than human and lunged for her.

Uncertain if it was Priest or something more sinister pretending to be him, Max opted to use non-lethal force, whipping the Shrike forward to bury it into his left shoulder—deep enough to strike bone. It took two tries to free the steel blade. By then, Priest was crashing into Max and the burning pain of sharp teeth followed, ripping into her throat and radiating to her skull like a hot wire.

Unleashing a scream of surprise and pain, Max tried to shove away, wedging the tomahawk between them to keep his teeth from sinking further, but it was like trying to move a brick wall. Smelling and then tasting her own blood on her lips, Max felt a spurt of alarm. Silently praying that they would both somehow survive this, she reached for the revolver and fired one shot into Priest's hip. The sound of gunfire blasted through the night, accompanied by a howl of pain as Priest released the deadly hold on her throat.

Crouching on the forest floor, Priest glared up at her with an evil, murderous stare, and Max didn't recognize him at all. With a sickening twist in her gut, she wondered if he had somehow contracted the same strain of rabies responsible for turning a once shy and mischievous tree giant into a rampant murderer.

She stumbled backward, clutching the gun in one trembling hand as the other touched the wound on her neck. Her hand came away slick with blood, and Max took another staggering step backward, dizzy from either blood loss or panic.

Rumbling a low, threatening growl, Priest began to crawl toward her even as Max begged him to stop. The one leg mangled by the gunshot dragged awkwardly behind him, leaving a heavy trail of blood. Max kept moving away as he advanced, keeping the gun level but knowing in her heart that she could never take the kill shot. Not on Priest.

"Just stop goddammit," she screamed.

Priest answered with a noise she'd never heard from him or any other soldier from his program. And then he was hurtling through the air with rage in his eyes and a mouthful of needle-sharp fangs. Shrieking, Max stupidly put her hands up to stop him. And that's when the light appeared—pure, golden, and brighter than even the moon—starting as a singular sphere of radiance and rapidly expanding. A low hum reached her ears, and then in an instant, the light exploded, funneling outward in one concentrated beam of power that impacted Priest square in the chest. He dropped like a stone, falling to the earth in a motionless heap with tendrils of smoke curling upward from his skin.

Oh shit. In total disbelief, Max stared at her hands, looked at Priest and then back at her hands. She shook her head. There wasn't time to dwell on why the hell, for the second time, golden pulses had suddenly emerged from her palms because Priest was already stirring. Racing over to his downed body, she pulled the hemlock-tipped handcuffs from her pocket and quickly snapped them around his wrists. Exhaling a shaky breath, she knelt next to him and tentatively called his name.

Priest couldn't have rabies. The timeline wasn't right. Even with the aggressive strain that had eclipsed the tree giant's mind, it had taken days for the virus to have such an effect. Max had been in constant contact with Priest for the past forty-eight hours. Surely, he would have mentioned being bitten by a potentially infected creature or shown some sign of illness. Unless the saurummut had somehow done this...

"Priest," she tried again.

His eyes opened, but took an extra moment before they focused on her face.

"Max," he said, speaking in a rasping hiss that sounded nothing like Priest.

Startled, Max shifted away, putting more distance between them.

"Max," he repeated. His voice, though still guttural, sounded less serpent-like.

She held her breath, not knowing what do, and tried to not to give in to the awful feeling pressing against her.

"Max," he said for a third time, and at last, she could hear Priest in there.

"What happened to you," she whispered.

Max swallowed. There was only one phone call she knew to make and hoped with all her heart that it would be the right one. Otherwise, Priest would end up in a specimen tank…or worse.

But as she reached for her phone, Priest underwent another frightening change, and Max's blood all but turned solid within her veins. A second iris melded from the first in each of his eyes, migrating to opposite ends of each orbit. The color of them evolved from blue to red, and then Priest was on his feet, tearing the handcuffs apart even as his wrists were shredded and bloodied by the spikes. Max looked on in complete horror, as skin began to fall from his face and body, dropping to the ground in steaming piles. He collapsed to all fours, and the sloughing persisted, revealing putrid greenish patches beneath. The crack of breaking bones overtook the sound of his flesh smacking wetly onto the forest floor.

Keeping her attention on the unbelievably gruesome transformation happening before her, Max dialed her father's number. "C'mon, c'mon," she urged as it continued to ring. When the call went to voicemail, Max hung up and dialed the second contact she had for him. Her dad had given it to Max back when she was a kid and miserable because Daddy was going away yet again. It was his absolutely-do-not-call, ~~even-if-the-house-is-on-fire~~ even-if-you-are-on-fire number. Her father had instructed Max to use it only if the world were actually ending. Having never called the number, Max thought it had been her father's way of reassuring a sad little girl that if she really and truly needed him, he was always within reach.

"I'm in trouble," she said when the voicemail switched on. "Track Priest's coordinates. You'll find us there." Max hesitated. "Please, Dad. I don't know what to do," she whispered. And then for good measure, she aimed the phone's speaker toward the awful noises coming from where Priest's body continued to contort and expand in size as he roared more fearsomely than any beast she had ever encountered.

As his spinal column realigned and settled, there was one final snap—as if a huge tree branch had broken away—then the thing that was once Priest raised its ghastly head, and Max was certain she had lost him forever.

"Oh no," she uttered in a choked whisper.

The thing crouching before Max was unrecognizable. Nothing came close to matching its grotesque appearance. Muscle was piled on top of muscle, giving the creature's body the appearance of a bull on steroids. The head was more canine in appearance—if a dog had fallen in a vat of toxic waste and mutated into something from the worst of nightmares. Huge veins, knotted and gnarled like spider webs, stretched everywhere across the greyish skin. Claws and teeth, clearly made for killing, dripped with black ooze.

Max didn't know when it happened; she only gradually became aware that she was no longer looking at the monster, but her legs were pumping, her feet pounding against the earth, carrying her as far away from the creature, as swiftly as possible. She didn't have a plan. Her immediate hope was to evade it long enough to circle back to the SUV, regroup and resupply.

She ran a mental catalogue of the non-lethal weapons at her disposal. There weren't many. She'd come to the mountainside thinking Priest was in trouble and was therefore prepared to kill whatever necessary to save him. Had she known Priest would be the very thing she would be fighting—well, Max would have taken different precautions.

Reaching into her belt, she pulled the tracker into view, extra careful of her feet while she calculated the red dot's trajectory. Max could hear creature-Priest crashing through the trees behind her, but oddly, the red dot hadn't moved. *Shit. Shit. Shit.* So much for that idea. Maybe the violent transformation had somehow damaged his implant. That would mean her father—if he decided to help—would take longer to find them.

That's okay. You're okay. Stay cool.

Max kept running, heart and lungs working harder as the landscape changed, muscles in her legs firing desperately as the elevation increased. No good. Steeper terrain would slow her down and put her at a disadvantage, allowing that thing to catch her within a quarter of a mile. Cutting to the right, Max angled her path away from the hillside. Immediately, a guttural roar bellowed from behind her, overtaking the night. Creature-Priest's pace intensified and the gap between them narrowed at an alarming rate.

With the heat of creature-Priest's breath practically caressing her neck like a whispering lover, Max spotted a narrow, hidden recess and had less than a split second to decide whether she had been herded to that very location before diving into the hollow. Both her left shoulder and elbow took a heavy battering against jutted rocks lining the cramped passage, barely wide enough for her to fit through, even while moving sideways. When the duffel of ammo snagged and wouldn't budge free, worry ripped through Max's brain. She couldn't get trapped there with no room to defend herself. Priest wasn't in control and would kill her in seconds. Cursing the decision even as she made it, Max cut the strap to the duffel and shoved forward.

She hadn't gone three feet when the passage narrowed further, shrinking the space between her skin and the sharp stone until none remained. But if she barely fit, there was no way creature-Priest ever would. The realization made Max feel marginally better about leaving the extra weaponry behind.

When the gap finally expanded, Max hurdled through, slamming her elbow against the rocky boundaries one last time. She dropped low and spun around, tomahawk in one hand and revolver in the other, chest heaving as she waited to see whether she had been wrong, if creature-Priest could actually follow. She wasn't willing to kill him to survive, but Max wouldn't hesitate to defend herself. Luckily, the tight crevice did bar the creature's monstrous girth from entry, and she watched with mounting relief and pity as it unleashed a furious onslaught against the rocks, clawing and biting savagely at the blockade protecting its intended prey. Ending as quickly as it began, the violence ceased, leaving an unnatural silence in its wake.

After a slight hesitation, Max holstered the revolver and once again reached for the tracker. She wasn't sure why. The damned thing had proven useless thus far. Taking another look at the screen, she saw the red dot's location indicated that Max was directly on top of it.

What the hell?

Switching on a small but powerful flashlight, Max turned in a slow circle. Damp and mossy cave walls stood on every side except one. Glancing at the tracker, she shifted her attention to the gaping hole of infinite darkness, un-pierceable even by the powerful halogen beam. It seemed that darkness was only her option if she hoped to see this thing through.

She had traveled for less than five minutes when the smell of rot hit her nostrils. With every step, the putrid odor only thickened until Max could actually taste decay on her tongue. Gagging, she used one sleeve to cover her nose and mouth, but the urge to retch remained constant. As Max continued forward, another scent hit her nose—one that struck fear inside her heart.

Blood. Stale blood. Fresh blood. Lots of blood.

And then Max began to see them. Bodies. Dozens—possibly a hundred or more—lined the cave floor, stacked in piles, and stretched out before her. All stages of decomposition were manifested. Some had bloated skin. Others were sunken and withered. There were young and old, male and female. A few wore what looked like suits. Some wore everyday casual jeans and sneakers. Others were naked. The killer of these people had shown no discretion. However, it was the freshest and bloodiest corpses that were the most terrifying.

These kills were dressed in all black, boots, and vests—the remnants of tactical gear. Their flesh had been torn to shreds. Throats ripped. Bones splintered. Limbs missing or partially detached. Skulls broken apart. Struggling to breathe, Max shined the light on each of them, but most of their faces had been mangled beyond recognition. Eyes were missing. Foreheads shredded. Jaws and noses crushed.

Hands quaking, Max checked the tracker. To her dismay, the red dot was still active and transmitting this exact location. Doubled over by the realization, she inhaled deeply, but the sound came out more as a strangled wheeze. Max knew if she didn't calm down, she would hyperventilate.

Over her own labored breathing, she heard someone call her name, and the sound sent ice through her veins. Straightening stiffly, Max shone the light in the direction of the voice…and there he was.

"Max," he called in a rasping whisper.

Priest. Oh god, Priest.

In human form once more, Priest watched her from across the scores of bodies. And she had never been more afraid of him—or for him.

"Priest, did you do this?"

He didn't reply but continued watching her. Caught in the flashlight's steady beam, his eyes glittered, reflecting a yellow night shine. Max clutched the tomahawk tighter as her resolve began to waver. Night shine was an animalistic trait not exhibited in soldiers engineered during Project Washington, so his eyes really should not have been doing that. On the other hand, Priest really *really* shouldn't have been able to transform into the horrid creature responsible for chasing her into a mass grave of mutilated victims. But the various stages of decay indicated that many of these people had died weeks ago.

Max adjusted her grip on the tomahawk, moving slowly to sheath it between her shoulders. *That's not Priest,* she decided, even as the agony of understanding threatened to rend her apart. More than likely, Priest was dead and his body located somewhere within the ghastly cornucopia of corpses. It was what the tracker had indicated all along.

A single tear welled up within Max's left eye. It was the sum of emotion she would allow herself to feel. And before the moisture had reached her cheek, she whipped the revolver from her hip and pulled the trigger. No more hesitation. This monstrosity could no longer go on existing.

Though her aim was perfect, creature-Priest was incredibly fast and *strong*. Its body jerked a full quarter-turn from the fifty-caliber impact, and then disappeared in blur of movement, crashing into Max, brutally pounding her down into the stone cave floor. Pain shot through her already injured neck and shoulder, reminding Max of her severe disadvantage in such close quarter combat. But she ignored the protests of her damaged body, grappling to leverage creature-Priest into an overhead toss. The flashlight had been knocked away, but its illumination remained, partially lighting the cavern. And as the creature regained its feet, Max sighted it, sparing a split second to fire the revolver again. Whether hit or miss, Max couldn't tell—the thing kept coming—far too quickly for her to take aim again. In the next second, it was on her and what felt like the torture of a dozen hot knives tore through Max's forearm and fingers, causing her to lose her grip on the revolver. Quickly drawing the Shrike with her opposite hand, Max struck out, chopping downward in two successive movements, aiming at what she hoped was the base of the creature's skull. Blood went everywhere, jetting out in chaotic streams of red to splatter hotly against her skin.

Releasing a rumbling growl from deep within its throat, the creature relinquished her and retreated into the darkness. Back and forth, it paced through the stream of light. It bared its teeth, and her blood dripped from its chin and lips. But the creature did not attack.

Max noted the gunshot wound to its hip had already seemed to have healed. She flexed the fingers of her right hand, testing them. The movement was both painful and severely limited. Even worse was the dimness rapidly encroaching on her field of vision. Max wasn't sure if it was because of the flashlight's shrinking glow or if she had lost too much blood. Either way, she needed to end this fight now.

She tried searching for the revolver without taking her gaze from the creature's disorienting movements, but the gun had fallen into obscurity. Max couldn't risk the vulnerability resulting from any attempt to find it.

That bag of ammo sure as hell would be handy right about now, she thought bitterly. She didn't regret putting Priest's welfare before her own. What sucked was that this thing wasn't Priest at all…and she had probably sacrificed herself for a homicidal monster.

Screw it, Max thought. Knowing her next move would likely provoke the creature to attack, she dropped low, keeping the Shrike ready while sweeping for the revolver with her injured hand. *So, it can heal one bullet wound. Let's see it try to heal ten.*

Just as she figured, creature-Priest charged from the darkness—partially human and headed toward her like a runaway train. Rolling sideways, Max brought the tomahawk up in a slicing motion and received a satisfying shower of the creature's blood. But her gratification was extremely short-lived. Creature-Priest turned in mid-air, redirecting its momentum in an incredible display of agility. Max swung the Shrike again and again, connecting each time to make it recoil in pain, but the thing was unstoppable. Sinking its claws into her thighs, it dragged her across the cave floor, pulling her toward its waiting fangs. Screaming, Max shoved the tomahawk into its mouth and wedged its jaws open with the steel blade. That was enough to make it release her, and Max scrambled away.

Both she and creature-Priest were pouring blood from their injuries. But now Max was weaponless, and creature-Priest still had several ways to kill her at its disposal.

She was out of options.

Lunging for the flashlight, Max turned and ran as fast as her damaged legs could manage—which wasn't very fast at all. She followed her nose, moving away from the smell of decay and hopefully toward the cramped passage exiting out of this nightmare and where the creature couldn't follow.

She staggered on, unable to hear or see her pursuer, not even knowing if it was there. Too afraid to stop and check her bearings, Max kept going in the direction she hoped was right. When the flashlight's beam discovered what looked like the narrow entrance, Max doubled her efforts to reach it. She was nearly there when agony encircled her ankle. Her injuries at last overtook her, legs buckling as she was thrown down to the rocky cave floor. The wind left her lungs in a whoosh. Her eyes lost the light. She couldn't move. Couldn't breathe. She could only listen helplessly to the enraged roar that sounded directly overhead. It was over.

And then a second, even more ferocious roar one answered. A series of snarls erupted, along with the sounds of a furious scuffle, echoing strangely within the cavern.

Clumsily grabbing for the flashlight, Max directed it toward the chaos and was almost unable to believe what she saw. Priest—the real Priest—grappled with the monster. From the way he moved, Max could tell he was terribly hurt and losing the struggle to keep the creature's jaws at bay.

Pushing to her feet, she collapsed again, gritting her teeth to suppress a cry because the agony was so incredible. Turning, Priest saw her trying to reach him and shook his head. *"Fall back,"* he yelled.

The sickening crunch of bone reached her ears, followed by Priest's muffled grunt of pain. And then his body was hurtling through the air, hitting the rocks before landing several feet beyond her position. The sight of his crumpled, unmoving form was enough to make Max forget her pain and the fact that her right leg wasn't really cooperating anymore.

She half-dragged, half-stumbled herself to him and dropped to her knees. Blood covered his face. Bite marks had shredded his shoulder and arm. He was conscious, but barely. Before she could speak, Priest opened one hand, exposing two gleaming metal pins of now active grenades. "Get out of here," he said weakly.

Fuck.

Reaching into a reserve of strength Max didn't know existed within her, she hauled Priest up by the tactical vest he wore and pulled him backward. Seconds later, an explosion tore through the cavern, blasting apart the walls and ceilings, sending an avalanche of rock and dirt down around them. She kept moving, even as burning heat scorched her skin and hair. She pushed aside the pain, ignored her body's pleas to quit. Reaching the opening, Max adjusted her grip on the vest and moved sideways, trying to keep momentum as the cave continued to collapse, dragging Priest's considerable weight with her. Several times, she was forced to stop and wedge him through areas where even she barely fit.

It was by the sheer force of her will that they made it out to breathe in the open air again. Crumpling to the ground, Max fought back but she was succumbing to the pain, to her injuries.

Don't pass out. Don't pass out.

Gritting her teeth, she kneeled next to Priest, but the leg that wouldn't work remained stretch out awkwardly as she leaned over his motionless form, anxiously calling his name. It took a second too long, but eventually, his eyes found hers. Only now they lacked their usual luster, staring at her—dim and unfocused. "Max," he murmured weakly. "What the hell…"

The sentence trailed, unfinished, as Priest's eyes closed and he drifted out of consciousness.

Swearing, Max unstrapped the armor-plated vest and gently peeled back the shirt underneath to check his wounds, but there was too much blood. She couldn't discern where it originated. His neck and shoulder were badly bitten, but those wounds weren't mortal.

Max removed her blouse, thinking she needed to get back to the SUV and retrieve the medical kit, but the vehicle was too far away. She couldn't leave Priest alone for that long. He was in too bad of shape. So, she did her best, using the fabric of her blouse to absorb enough blood to locate the source of his injuries.

What she found was shocking—two exit points on his chest and abdomen. For bullets to penetrate the level of body protection worn by UCC operators, the munitions would have to be explosive and armor-piercing. Max blotted the wounds again to be sure, and Priest flinched away from her touch. His already ashen skin paled even more.

"Priest," she called softly as his eyes fluttered opened. "These are bullet holes."

He licked his lips. "Yeah. Hauser shot me."

Hauser—she remembered that name. He had been one of the two assholes who'd tried to force her into a strip search. "Friendly fire? From behind?" She had to be sure.

Priest choked out a weak laugh, ejecting a frothy stream of blood onto his lips. "Didn't feel so friendly," he said. "It wasn't his fault. Hauser was trying to survive. That thing…" He paused as he struggled for enough air to continue. "It was a juvenile…learning to hunt…learning to be human. Feeding on victims…acquiring their memories, so it could—" His entire face contorted with pain, and then he stopped breathing.

"It's okay," she insisted. "You're okay."

Max lifted the makeshift bandage—heavy and soaked through with blood. Both bullets had hit major arteries. It was obvious from the blood's dark color and the force with which it was expelled from his body. His clammy skin grew even colder—now icy to the touch. Unless Max could slow the bleeding, Priest didn't have much time.

"Sorry about this," she whispered. Then Max reached into his chest with her remaining good hand and searched for the bleeding artery. Her heart ached for him as he whimpered in pain, suppressing the scream she would have never been able to cage had their roles been reversed. A small torrent surged over her fingers with every beat of his heart, alerting Max that she had found the bleed. But the artery had retracted from reach. Wincing, she dared to explore deeper. At last locating the wayward artery, she clamped her fingers around it and applied constant pressure. Priest shuddered. Making a strangled noise, his entire body lifted upward as if trying to flee from the pain.

"I got it, Priest," she said, attempting to soothe him. "But you have to stay still."

Priest's throat worked, laboring to execute a singular swallow. He nodded.

"Okay," Max whispered. "Okay."

Of course, her nose started to itch then. Max didn't give it a second thought. Noticing a considerable amount of blood still oozing from the wound, she applied more pressure, counting the seconds and then minutes until the outpour progressively slowed.

Priest's eyes had closed, and shifted beneath his twitching eyelids. When she called to him, they slowly opened. Bearing a distant gaze, he looked at her. His mouth worked, but no sound came out. Max was about to tell him not to speak and to save his strength. Then he whispered her name. "Max." He spoke so softly that she could barely hear him.

Relief slightly loosened the tightness in her chest. "You're going to be okay," Max said firmly. She shoved back the dread and panic when the useless emotions strained to break free of her bravado façade.

She considered the other wound in his abdomen. It was bad. Really bad. An enormous pool of blood collected beneath Priest's body. It was a wonder he still lived at all. She knew it could only be the strength from his genetic enhancement that had kept him alive for so long.

Releasing the pressure inside his chest was out of the question. Plus, her right hand had gone fully numb, but Priest wouldn't survive much longer if she didn't do something about the hole in his stomach.

"You're still bleeding badly and I have to stop it." She hesitated. "Priest, this is going to hurt."

"Max, don't," he said weakly. "I can't—"

The rest of his sentence became an agonized, gut-wrenching cry of pain when she planted her knee into his abdomen and used her weight to apply enough compression to stop the bleeding. His face turned ghostly white. He gritted his teeth, cutting off the scream as his body convulsed beneath the agony Max inflicted upon him. Rooting her body to his, she didn't ease up. In time, the spasms calmed. His breathing became shallow and strained. His hands trembled, but he was alive. He was still with her.

"I'm so sorry."

Exhaling forcefully, Priest swallowed. "Fuck," he gasped.

"I know. Just hang on. Help is coming."

"Make sure…they recover the bodies. And match DNA with missing victims. Sweep the area…confirm there isn't another…one of those things."

Max shook her head. "No. That's your job."

Priest watched her sadly. "I'm not…getting out of here." He smiled. "It was always you, Maxima. You gave me a different purpose…besides the killing." Shuddering, he labored through another ragged breath.

She wanted to look away—couldn't see straight through the tears anyway—but forced herself hold to his gaze. Priest was right. Despite her efforts, he was dying. A terrible pain swelled within her chest, increasing in size and heaviness until Max thought her ribs were going to explode outward. She vaguely wondered if this was what a breaking heart felt like.

"Harrison, don't," she begged. "Please stay with me."

"You'll be okay…Maximum."

And then, expelling one final sigh, Priest stopped breathing.

A scream tore from Max's throat. An animalistic sound, unfamiliar to her own ears. Beneath the mind-numbing grief, she became aware of the faint throb of blood still pulsing between her fingers. The force of each beat grew weaker and the gap between them wider as Priest's pulse slowed. Soon, his heart would stop altogether, like his breathing.

No.

She would not let this happen.

No.

Priest. Couldn't. Die.

NO.

Crying out, Max unleashed her anguish, fear, and anger onto the night, channeling it all into one wretched wail of grief. Then she reached inward, seeking within the very cells of her existence for the power to keep him on this earth, as if it were possible to *will* Priest to live. Letting out an anguished moan, she begged him to stay one final time. *"Please!"* she shouted.

The answer Max received was incredible.

Starting as a faint shimmer, a golden light began to emit from within Priest's chest. The glow intensified, deepening in color to become a dark bronze highlighted by strands of a radiant yellow. From the sky above, a deep growl of thunder boomed as huge clouds that weren't there a moment before suddenly took on an ominous formation, rolling and thickening as the thunder continuously rumbled.

A hue of the same bronze radiated from within the cloud mass, flashing brighter with each thunderous resonance, growing in force until a circle of light formed and tunneled downward to illuminate Max, Priest, and everything within a one-hundred-foot radius of their position.

The light within Priest began to pulsate. And then as unexpectedly as it had appeared, the light vanished. Quiet embraced the night, stretching out into several long seconds of utter silence, only to be shattered by a clap of thunder that sounded like splitting boulders. At the same time, some invisible force rippled through Priest, moving his entire body in one undulating motion. Max couldn't see it, but she felt the power flow through her as well.

Abruptly, the light stopped flashing. The thunder vanished. And the clouds settled, slowly dissipating into thin wisps to be swiftly carried away by a stiff wind.

And finally…

Priest breathed.

In one extended, gasping breath, his lungs stretched. His back arched as his fingers dragged through the dirt. And both of his hands clenched into fists. Coughing, he breathed again. And again. His heartbeat strengthened with every second. Still, Max didn't let go.

Priest opened his eyes. "Max?"

She wanted to kiss him, but didn't dare move. Constant pressure had to be maintained on his injuries. Sobbing through a short laugh, Max nodded. "I'm here."

Priest looked all around them. His expression was one of total confusion. "Do you hear that?"

Max frowned. She didn't hear anything other than the sweet sound of his lungs breathing air once more. Didn't feel anything except the renewed strength of his heartbeat. Fine tuning her senses beyond those two miracles, Max eventually discerned the rhythmic chopping of approaching helicopter blades. She grinned. "He came."

Thirteen

Even by physical standards alone, Maximillian "Mad Max" Masters was an imposing guy. Though well into his fifties, he maintained an impressive physique and a visage youthful enough to belong to someone in his late thirties. His dark brown hair was shaped in a traditional military style, but the black and grey camouflage he wore set him apart from the rest of the soldiers—as did the rank of Lieutenant Colonel. Lt. Col. Masters oversaw the workings of the entire UCC base where Priest's unit was assigned. He was on the top tier of officers within the Unified Combatant Command and had a special security clearance that probably exceeded what POTUS was entitled to.

Ten years ago, when he was still climbing the ranks, the importance of his position had made being a full-time father to Max virtually impossible. As a little girl, it had been difficult for Max to comprehend why her daddy wasn't around like the other dads. But now she understood—probably a little too well.

Lt. Col. Masters and his base of operatives were the first and final line of defense against whatever threat came through the interdimensional rifts. His job was a 24/7 undertaking. And no matter what, the mission always came first.

Max had moved aside to let the medical team tend to Priest's injuries, watching them intently while also scanning the sea of uniforms in search of her father. It wasn't until Priest was declared stable that her father—flanked by two burly and rather serious-looking operatives—strode onto the scene.

Struggling to her feet, Max pulled herself together and stood as tall as possible. She imagined how awful she must have looked and chewed her lip with regret. Her father wore a stern but worried expression as he approached, stopping a few feet short of her position to inspect her from head to toe.

"Why didn't you see a medic?" he demanded.

"My wounds are healing fast enough," she said, though thinking a hospital bed and a saline drip were exactly what she needed.

Dismissing his two companions with a single look, her father moved closer, pulling Max into his arms to place a tender kiss on her forehead. Exhausted and in pain, she wanted nothing more than to close her eyes and lean into his strength, especially after such a harrowing night, but her father had already stiffened and gently pushed her away. That brief show of affection would be the only indication of any familial bond between them as he shifted seamlessly back into the commanding persona of Lieutenant Colonel.

"What are you doing out here, Marshal? This is an active investigation and far outside of your jurisdiction."

Max was too tired to even roll her eyes. "I came to help Priest. He was in trouble."

Lt. Col. Masters crossed his arms. "And how exactly did you know that?"

Shit. "Uh," Max stammered. There was no way in hell she could tell him about the visions she'd been having...or the warning from the strange creature with serpent eyes. So, she revealed a different truth—one that might have an equally upsetting effect. "I've been staying with Priest for the past couple of nights. When he didn't come home tonight, I got worried and tracked him down."

"Is that so?" The colonel's frown deepened. "You two are supposed to be over."

Max scowled. While her father had never approved of her dating one of his soldiers, something about his phrasing rubbed her in the wrong way. "We aren't together," she snapped. "So relax."

"You don't give the orders here, Maxima."

She did roll her eyes then. "Right," she said, looking away from him.

"Sir," one of the soldiers called, claiming the colonel's attention.

"Go ahead and prep First Sergeant Preesti for questioning."

"What?" Max all but shouted. "He needs surgery. Why aren't you taking him to a hospital?"

When the soldier hesitated, looking between Max and her father, the colonel gave him a look that could have iced over the Sahara. "You have your orders," he said evenly. Taking Max by the arm, he escorted her a good thirty feet farther from the area, forcing her to adopt an awkward, painful limp just to keep up. "Priest's body is in shock. Somehow, the bastard is conscious, but he's critical, Max. He could very well die as soon as we put him under, so I need to know everything he knows before that happens. He must be debriefed first. I know you don't like it, Maxima. I don't like it either. But that is how things are. This is what he signed up for."

Max snatched away from him. "This may be what *you* signed up for, but Priest didn't sign up for anything. He never had a choice in any of this shit."

"Don't be unreasonable, Maxima."

"Unreasonable?" Her voice climbed two octaves with incredulity. "You just admitted that Priest could die. You may not care about that, but I do. Dad, I really care about him. So, fuck your debrief. If something happens to him…" her voice broke, forcing her to pause. Then she

swallowed that fear and finished the threat in a tone cold enough to rival even her father's. "I will *never* speak to you again. And you will never see me again."

The colonel's jaw clenched and unclenched. Fury practically exuded from his pores. His mood would have sent the most seasoned soldiers scampering for cover, but Max held firm, meeting her father's ire with an unwavering gaze.

Turning stiffly on his heel, the colonel stalked away from her without a second glance, gruffly barking new orders to the soldiers surrounding Priest. "Get him to the chopper, goddammit. We move out in five."

Max exhaled, staggering forward with the sheer amount of relief that spread throughout her body, but jerked in surprised when her father called her name. "Maxima," he said brusquely, "You will have dinner with me tomorrow night at eighteen hundred."

"Yes, sir," she whispered.

"Do you need a lift or do you have your own ride out of here?"

"I'm good." After a tiny hesitation, Max smiled. "Thank you," she added.

Giving a curt nod, her father turned away.

*

It was much worse than Max had imagined. Standing naked in front of a full-length mirror that hung in Priest's bedroom, she examined her injuries. Several ugly gashes on her neck and leg glared back, the skin puckered and raised as damaged flesh struggled to knit together. Extensive bruising covered her torso, hip, both legs and shoulders. Smaller cuts and scrapes marred her face. Blood, dirt, leaves, and mud encrusted every square inch of skin. Her hair was a tangled mess. And she was pretty sure that her right hand had sustained multiple fractures.

Stepping into the shower, Max washed her hair as best she could and rinsed her skin, enduring the sting as the warm water punished the open cuts all over her body. She took a bath next, soaking for over an hour in tub filled with hot water, lavender oil, and Epsom salt. Her brain wanted to be busy—wondering anxiously about Priest's condition, where and when she would see the strange golden-eyed creature again, what the consequences would be for attacking Dutch, if her dad would actually show up for dinner tomorrow night, and how Arabella's hot date had gone—but Max was simply too tired.

It was the shivering of her own body that awoke her—trying to preserve warmth in a bath that had turned cold long ago. Max checked the clock. She had been asleep for more than three hours.

Stiffly rising from the tub, she toweled off and threw on a bathrobe. It was Priest's and therefore way too large for her, but it was warm and smelled like him. Shuffling back to the bedroom, Max collapsed on top of the comforter and had about five seconds to contemplate what she would wear to work come morning since her only change of clothing had been torn to shreds and she still wasn't allowed to go back to her apartment. Then she fell into a deep, dreamless sleep. Night and most of the morning passed before a familiar voice tugged her from oblivion.

"You're going to be late."

Max opened her eyes to find Kuro calmly perched at the edge of Priest's king-sized bed. Disoriented at first, Max scrambled upright and executed a panicky check of her surroundings. Memories from the prior night came flooding back, only adding to her anxiety.

"Relax, Goldilocks. The creature that attacked you last night is gone. Those assholes from the UCC are still gathering all the pieces you and Priest left out there."

"That's good," Max managed, knowing she needed to say something or else Kuro would worry, but it was hard to think around the splitting headache that currently hammered against her skull.

"He pulled through surgery."

Swinging her legs to the side of the bed, Max pressed her hands to her face. One mention of Priest and she threatened to fall apart. Discreetly wiping her eyes, she cleared the lump from her throat and stood up. "That's really good. You think they'll let me see him?"

Kuro shook her head slowly. "For some reason, he's being kept under a four-man guard. No visitors in or out." The she-wolf tilted her head slightly to one side, while a hint of a smile played her lips. "You could, of course, ask the colonel to give you special clearance. I heard you called the old man on his shit last night."

Max winced. "I'm going to live to regret that."

Kuro's voice softened, surprising Max. "Have no regrets. You got Priest help when he needed it most."

Max ducked her face to hide the blush. "Right." Tying the bathrobe tighter around her waist, she paced the room—partly out of agitation, but mostly to stretch achy muscles.

"Here," Kuro said, momentarily distracting Max. "I thought you might need these."

Seeing the bag of clothing Kuro set on the bed, Max could have hugged the she-wolf. "You're a lifesaver."

"It was actually Tanaka's idea."

"Oh." Max took note of Kuro's flat expression and decided not to ask for elaboration. "I will be sure to thank him then." Taking the bag, she emptied its contents and started to dress, tugging on a fresh pair of panties and black denim leggings beneath the robe. "How did things go for you last night? Dutch give you trouble?"

"No," Kuro answered simply.

Okay. Max nodded and turned, putting her back to Kuro as she removed the robe and pulled on a sports bra. The garment belonged to Arabella and was a tad bit loose, but it got the job done.

"Ouch," Kuro said without any inflection of sympathy. "How are you even standing right now?"

Glancing down at her battered and bruised skin, Max shrugged. She'd forgotten her body looked like someone had tried to shove it through a blender. "I have a high pain tolerance and a massive stubborn streak."

Max set about deciding on a shirt to complete the work getup. Jensen had thoughtfully sent over several options, but in the end, Max selected a simple, oversized grey and black baseball t-shirt. She was pretty sure she'd left a spare jacket bearing the agency's official insignia at the office. With it, her outfit would seem completely professional. Tying her hair into a high, unruly ponytail, she sat down to lace up her boots and Kuro finally spoke again.

"You need to be careful, Max. You and Priest may have eliminated whatever was terrorizing this city, but someone—something—else was watching you last night."

Max's eyes widened in alarm. "Who?"

"Director Cranke's killer."

"So, you know who the killer is?"

"No," Kuro said carefully. "I didn't see him...only got his scent. He's like a ghost—even to my senses."

"Shit," Max muttered to herself as she processed a sudden revelation.

"You don't you seem surprised."

Max got up abruptly, intending to gather her weapons and head to the agency, but both the revolver and the Shrike had been casualties in the fight against the shapeshifter. The loss hurt more than the collective of her healing injuries.

"Kuro, I need a favor," Max said, not really acknowledging the she-wolf's statement. "Keep that tidbit of information to yourself for as long as possible. And if you absolutely have to tell someone, don't let it be Priest or my father."

"What's going on?"

Max shook her head. "Nothing I can't handle."

I'm so screwed, she added silently.

*

It was utterly mind-boggling to think of how much had transpired since Friday night. Dropping the kapre report into the interim director's mailbox, Max struggled to wrap her head around it. Still tired, sore, and in desperate need of an actual day off, she dreaded the moment when her new boss would call her in to review the report. Max wasn't sure she could trust her exhausted mind to omit the necessary details, dodge potentially compromising questions, or recount the encounter exactly as it was portrayed in a report that played fast and loose with actual facts.

A few hours later, when Max was summoned to the captain's office, she stood from her desk with a resigned sigh and marched through double steel doors and into the sequestered offices of USMPS. Standing from behind a huge oak desk as soon as Max walked in, Cpt. Knox offered a tiny hand that matched her petite frame. Even in high heels, the woman barely crossed five feet in height. However small in stature, Cpt. Knox managed to have a commanding presence from the way she carried herself, articulated her thoughts, and with the impeccable manner in which she dressed. Her pantsuit was perfectly tailored to fit her diminutive form. And the rose-colored blouse she wore, complemented by a beige and pink scarf, contrasted nicely with her skin tone. She was the textbook embodiment of elegance, authority, and femininity.

"Maxima Masters, how nice to officially meet you," she said as Max shook her extended hand. "I've been reading through Director Cranke's reports. Your name was mentioned on more than one occasion, and it has become clear to me that the late director thought highly of you, regarding you as a decidedly skilled marshal—even if at times brash and reckless."

"Um, thank you," Max said, though she wasn't too sure about the backhanded compliment.

"No thanks necessary, Marshal. I simply call it as I see it." She gestured to the chair situated before her desk. "Have a seat."

Once Max had obeyed, Knox continued standing and casually folded her arms across her chest. Her line of questioning then bulldozed in a direction that indicated she was done with the pleasantries. "Why don't you have a partner?"

"There are many marshals who don't have partners," Max answered easily.

"All other female marshals at this agency do," Knox fired back.

Max took a moment to bury her annoyance before answering. "That may be true, but to my knowledge, it's not an actual requirement. I prefer to work alone, Captain Knox. That preference has never adversely impacted my job performance."

"Yet," Knox amended, narrowing her eyes. "It hasn't affected your job performance yet. I read the kapre statement, Marshal. You were almost in over your head."

Hell, I didn't know the thing could camouflage itself to be invisible. No one did, Max thought. "You're right," she said aloud. "I ultimately made the mistake of pursuing the tree giant without the proper resources at my disposal." *Because I was on a date...in a fucking miniskirt...and without the rest of my toys.*

"And you realize that we would have preferred the kapre's capture alive?"

"Yes, but he would have died anyway. The strain of rabies Nihilson had contracted was incurable." *Unless you wanted to experiment on him.*

Knox pursed her lips and nodded. "Very well then. I'll honor the precedent Director Cranke has in place and not mandate that you take a partner. However, consider your circumstance as a subject of ongoing review. This agency has already lost one marshal this year, and it will not happen again under my watch."

"Thank you," Max said in all sincerity. If her solitary work ethic was the only thing Knox questioned about that bogus report, then Max considered it a lucky break. She decided to push the good fortune a tad further. "What's going to happen to Cute Kevin—ah—Kevin Beothuk?"

"The wendigo?" Knox asked, but Max doubted whether the captain actually needed clarification.

"Yes, the wendigo," Max agreed anyway.

"Not only did Mr. Beothuk break the law by not registering his species with immigration, but he committed a secondary federal offense in concealing that information during the application for a position within a government agency." Knox frowned. "Did you know about Mr. Beothuk's secret identity?"

"I did not."

"And what do you think should be done with him?"

All bristles on the inside, Max made it a point to keep her exterior completely calm. "Everyone makes mistakes, Captain. Kevin is a nice guy and a great worker. I think he should be allowed to stay."

"Apparently, you're not the only one," Knox muttered.

"Excuse me?"

"First Sergeant Preesti requested leniency on Kevin Beothuk's behalf. He personally vouched for him, in fact. Said that he would consider it a personal favor if I were to able to negotiate a full pardon for Mr. Beothuk and allow him to continue working at this agency. I was going to dismiss Preesti's appeal, but given his current condition, I have reconsidered." For the first time since Max had entered Knox's office, the interim director showed signs of having a soft side to her steely exterior. "How is Priest?"

Max's fingers reflexively dug into the armrest. "He made it out of surgery. Hopefully, I'll be allowed to see him soon."

Cpt. Knox nodded. "He's strong."

"I know," Max agreed softly.

Fourteen

After work, Max drove straight to the base with hopes of being granted access to see Priest. Though two new warrants had been issued for a couple of wayward paranormals, Max passed on both opportunities. Her body needed at least another day of healing before taking on any more bad guys. She also needed to replace her favorite weapons. Until then, she would continue to raid Priest's stash.

Earlier in the day, Max Sr. had made a rare phone call to his only daughter. It was an amicable conversation, lasting just long enough to confirm plans for dinner. Max wanted to wager that her father might be in a good enough mood to ease the security protocols surrounding Priest's recovery, but the lieutenant colonel was hardly a man of leniency. And at the first hint that romance had blossomed between his daughter and one of his grunts again, any good mood of his would be dispelled. Of course, none of that meant Max wasn't going to try.

Passing through initial checkpoints to gain access to the base was simple enough. Still driving Priest's military issued SUV, Max even had access to employee parking. The first hitch only came as she walked to the medical building and spotted Dutch. Max tried to discreetly alter her course to ensure their paths did not cross, but as soon as she did, Dutch moved to quickly intercept. Since there was no way to avoid him without making a scene, Max muttered an oath under her breath and stopped. Dutch stood in front her, smiling down at Max as if they were old friends. She tried not to stare at the ugly bruising that surrounded his nose and bled outward to the skin beneath his eyes. "Hiya there, sweetcheeks," he said.

Max scowled. Sore, sleep-deprived, and worried about Priest, she really didn't feel like being hassled. "Do you remember what happened the last time you called me sweetcheeks? If not, go look in a mirror."

Dutch winked. "I work for your father, so I'm used to pain. And sometimes," he lowered his voice and edged closer. "I even like it."

"Ugh." Max quickly maneuvered away from him. "What do you want, Dutch?"

"An apology."

"No chance." She moved to walk past him, but he stepped in front of her, blocking the way.

"I didn't mean from you, sweetcheeks."

Max gritted her teeth. "What are you talking about?"

"Last night, Priest needed me and I wasn't there." He stared down at the pavement, thoughtfully rubbing his jaw. "I was too busy being an errand boy for the colonel." Dutch fell silent, seemingly lost in his own thoughts, and Max—unsure of what to say—let the quiet stretch between them.

When Dutch's stormy gaze met hers again, his expression reflected the anger in those dark blue eyes. "I'm glad you kicked my ass and went after him. He might not still be with us if you hadn't. So, I'm the one who's sorry."

"Oh," Max said. Thoroughly surprised, she ran short on words. This was officially the least unsettling conversation she'd ever held with Carter Lasseter.

"I didn't tell the colonel what happened last night, and I won't. But I'd watch myself if I were you, Max. You may be daddy's little girl, but the colonel will let nothing stop his mission." He moved out of her way. "That's all now."

Finally free to enter the medical facility, Max should have hurried inside, but something held her in place. She blew out a long a breath. "Thanks for the warning, Dutch." *That's two in one day.* Max hesitated. "And sorry about your nose."

"No worries, sweetcheeks. Us Washington boys can take some punishment." He gave her another slow wink. "Those boys on guard won't give you any trouble. I already told 'em you were coming," he drawled. "Priest ain't talking, but he's in there. Tell that asshole to hurry up and get his limp dick out of bed." Then Dutch abruptly turned, softly whistling a disjointed tune as he strode away.

Shaking her head thoughtfully, Max jogged up the stairs to the medical center while wondering if Dutch had really managed to bypass the red tape, making it possible for her to see Priest. Maybe, just maybe, she had been too hard on the guy all this time.

A blast of chilled air hit her as she passed through the automated doors and beneath one of several atmospheric curtains installed throughout many entry and exits points within the building, designed to reduce energy loss and prevent contaminants from escaping. A severe-looking soldier looked up from behind a desk located next to the elevators. Wary eyes considered Max with a mixture of boredom and suspicion. Max understood. Though healing, make-up couldn't hide the extensive bruising on her face and neck. Her dress was pretty casual, and the emblem of USPMS stitched into her jacket carried no authority on base. This corporal would be the first hurdle to gaining access to Priest.

Striding up to the desk like she belonged there, Max introduced herself and announced the reason for her visit. "Maxima Masters," she said, taking a slight pause to allow the corporal time to process that her last name was identical to that of the man who commanded the entire base. Normally, doing such a thing would have made

Max feel like a complete asshole. But these were exceptional circumstances. "I'm here to see First Sergeant Harrison Preesti," she finished.

The corporal punched a few strokes without delay and studied her monitor. Then she gave Max an apologetic look. "Preesti is in room nine-one-nine. I can buzz you up, but that area is a restricted floor. I don't know if you'll be able to see him."

Max had already moved to the elevator. She turned, glancing at the corporal over one shoulder. "I'll be fine," she said, and then quickly stepped inside once the doors opened.

She didn't have to read any room numbers to know where Priest was being held. The four-man guard stationed outside of his door was enough of a clue. Her stomach was a ball of nerves as she approached the soldiers, but remembering Dutch's promise somewhat tempered that anxiety.

Two of the men held fully automatic weapons strapped across their chests while the others only carried side arms. Dressed in light body armor, all four stood at full attention. On seeing Max, one of the men inclined his head in a fractional movement. Then he and the soldier next to him stepped aside. "We don't rotate out until morning," he said. "Take your time, ma'am."

"Thank you," Max said. Dragging in a deep breath, she opened the door and entered Priest's room.

The first thing she noticed was how small he seemed, his unmoving form partially covered beneath stark white sheets, with half a dozen tubes and wires connecting him to an array of blinking, humming equipment. Thick bandages covered most of his torso. Saline bags hung next to the bed, infusing his veins with fluids, while a constant stream of oxygen nourished deprived cells.

Edging closer, she could see remnants of blood on his skin. A gritty mixture of blood and soil lingered beneath his nails and darkened his light-blond, usually perfectly coiffed locks. He was so pale and still, that if not for the rise and fall of his chest, Max would have thought he was dead.

Max knew little about medicine, but basic vital signs were well within the realms of her understanding. His pulse was steady—if a little too fast. Blood pressure was low but passable. As for his oxygen levels—Max wasn't certain, but eighty-two percent seemed inadequate. Additionally, she saw two other monitors tracking things she had no idea about.

Max held his hand, happy to be near him and able to touch him again. She thought of all the things yet to be said between them while hoping for another chance to say them. Tasting salt on her lips, Max realized she was crying.

"It seems like I've been doing that a lot lately," she whispered.

The door opened and Max turned to see a man enter the room. Late forties, wearing dark-rimmed glasses that dominated everything else except a kind smile that radiated warmth, the man held a clipboard against his chest. "I'm Doctor Thorne, Harrison's attending physician."

"What's wrong with him?" Max asked, seeing no reason not to bypass any small talk.

Dr. Thorne nodded as if understanding. "The bullets severed major arteries in both Harrison's abdominal and thoracic cavities, resulting in tremendous blood loss—over two-thirds of it to be frank. Even now, I'm not sure how he survived more than a few minutes with those injuries. Even a soldier of his caliber—with his superior genetic makeup—should have died." Dr. Thorne shook his head. "You were first on the scene, so whatever measures you took must have played a huge part in saving his life."

Max didn't like the way the doctor was watching her, and he seemed too eager for her response. "I only applied pressure to his wounds, doctor. Nothing unusual, unless you consider reaching inside his chest to clamp a bleed extraordinary."

"Okay. Right." Dr. Thorne scratched his head. "By the time we got him into surgery, his vitals were well out of survivable ranges. His body had entered a severe state of shock. We gave him fluids and three blood transfusions, but I'm afraid that Harrison's organs were without sufficient oxygen for far too long. He's being heavily sedated until we can figure out exactly how extensive the damage is." Dr. Thorne pointed to one of the beeping monitors. "This screen displays Harrison's brain activity in real time. As you can see, there is very little." His voice softened. "We can't risk reviving a Project Washington subject who has brain damage. He has to show us he's in there. And he has to do it on his own."

As the doctor spoke, Max's mouth had gotten progressively drier, reaching the point where swallowing became painful. "How long does he have?" she asked, knowing that because the UCC saw Priest as property rather than an actual person, there would be special limitations.

Dr. Thorne's expression pinched as if he were suddenly uncomfortable. He ducked his head before answering. "He has thirty-six hours, and then UCC protocols mandate immediate termination."

"And there's nothing you can do?"

"I'm afraid not. I really am sorry, but it's up to Harrison now."

Squeezing Priest's hand harder, Max studied him wistfully, wishing with her whole heart that she possessed the power to will him out of that hospital bed. At some point, Dr. Thorne quietly left the room, leaving her alone with those impossible yearnings.

Only a couple of hours remained before she was due to meet her father for dinner, and Max intended on spending every second of that time with Priest. Dragging a chair to his bedside, she sat down and pulled the latest issue of *Bass Strings* from her messenger bag.

"I was going to bring an actual book—one of those self-indulgent autobiographies that you always have your nose stuck in—but then I realized trying to read that crap aloud would only be torture for the both of us." She opened the magazine to two random, glossy pages and read in a cheery tone, "Intra- and Interbrain Synchronization: How Guitarists' Brains Differ from Other Musicians." Max stopped, groaning inwardly. "This might actually be worse." Flipping back to the front cover, she considered the closeup shot of an instrument similar to an acoustic guitar in Priest's collection—artistically quartered and overlaid with several filters. Deciding the artwork was an incredibly misleading representation of the expected material, Max regretted not choosing an autobiography. "Okay, here goes."

Plodding through that article, she moved on to the next, infusing as much interest as she could into her reading. Accompanied by the constant hum of hospital machinery, only her voice filled the silence. She was surprised to find herself gradually absorbed in the pages, lured in by the prospect of gaining a better understanding of something Priest loved and the slightest chance of reaching him through it.

The chime of her wristwatch sounded, startling Max from her reading. It was time for the dinner date with her father. Standing up, she languished in a generous stretch, freshly rediscovering the lingering ache of her injuries.

Taking his hand one last time, she leaned over and kissed his lips ever so gently. "Priest," she whispered, "It's time to wake up."

The monitors began beeping erratically, their displays shifting to reflect simultaneous, but incremental, increases in heart rate, respiration, and blood pressure. Max froze and held her breath. Just as quickly, all of the values returned to sub-normal levels.

"Priest, please," she begged. Now, only thirty-four hours remained for him to prove himself useful to the UCC. "Wake up. I need you."

Fifteen

"Let's just call these I'm-sorry-for-being-a-terrible-parent presents," Lt. Col. Masters said, passing a large gift bag across the table and into Max's hands.

It was heavy, pink and purple, and stuffed to the brim with fluffy tissue paper. Max raised a skeptical eyebrow. "Should I open it now or wait?"

Smiling sheepishly, her father scanned the restaurant and shrugged his broad shoulders. "Later is probably better."

Wearing khakis, a white button-down shirt, and tennis shoes, Maximillian Masters had the appearance of a much younger man. Max was well aware that the average civilian had a hard time believing he was old enough to be her father. Without the stuffy uniform or the severity that uniform demanded, her father almost became a different person. Back when Max was a little girl, she lived for moments when she could see her father like this.

The dinner spot he chose was a fancy Italian bistro called Luca's. Often booked for months in advance, entrees started at three times what Max could afford. Appetizer prices were equally laughable. Since her father was paying, Max made a special effort not to chew her nails or worry about how astronomical the bill would be as she considered what to order. She sipped a generous pour of Chianti as they waited for the antipasto, trying to relax and enjoy some light conversation between them. Her gut knew the tone would soon change.

Cue the colonel.

"I heard you got past security and saw Priest today."

Here we go. Max took a long swallow of wine. "I did," she finally said, deciding there was no point in denying it.

"Any change?"

She stared at the white tablecloth as she answered. "I don't think so."

"Are you prepared for what has to happen if he doesn't improve?"

She nodded, but her throat tightened. "Do we have to talk about this?"

"I need to make sure my girl is going to be okay. Maxima, I can't have you falling apart again."

Temper flaring, Max looked up and met her father's gaze with an indignant glare. "Then why don't you stop it? They're going to put Priest down like he's no better than a sick animal."

"I can't stop that. Not even for you, Maximum." He sighed. "This is why I've always tried my damnedest to keep you away from all of this—why I never wanted you getting involved with Priest. His world is different from yours, Max. It's much harsher. I know Priest seems human to you, but really he's not."

"You're wrong about that," she interjected angrily.

"No. Listen to me. Project Washington's fatal flaw was in its extreme science. They created something that looks, feels, and sounds human—but the emotion isn't there, Maxima. There's no conscience or moral compass. No soul. Every soldier engineered from that experiment was a weapon. When Command lost control of them, those weapons became monsters that had to be eliminated. Through decisive action, we barely avoided catastrophe."

Max gritted her teeth. "Priest is different. That's why he wasn't killed with the rest. He's been so loyal to you all these years," she said, shaking her head. "I can't understand how you could just turn your back on him now."

"Okay, Max. I didn't want to hurt you, but you're just not hearing me. So, I'm going to stop sugarcoating this shit." Her father paused as the waiter returned to refill their wine glasses, his jaw clenching, his hand fisted with frustration. When the waiter left, he wasted no time driving home the point. "Priest does not love you. He is a weapon, guided and controlled solely by the orders he is given. He built this pretense of caring about you because that is what he was told to do." Her father's eyes hardened, bearing the coldness usually reserved for personnel under his command. "Because that is what I told him to do," he finished.

The entire time he spoke, Max kept telling herself that she wouldn't let her father get under her skin. She kept imagining happier times between them, before he became this stranger in uniform. But every word he said stung more deeply than the last, and without Max ever being cognizant of moving from her chair, she suddenly stood over the lieutenant colonel, staring down at him with more rage than she'd felt in a long time.

"I think it's better for us both if I leave now," Max said quietly, surprised by the perfect calm contained within her voice. "All this talk of monsters…sometimes, I think you forget about the part of me that isn't human."

"Maxima," her father said slowly, looking down where her fingertips tensely dug into the table's surface. "What's happening?"

She followed his gaze and was aghast to see the strange, bronze glow emitting from beneath her palms. *Shit.* Balling both hands into fists, Max ignored his question and stormed out of the restaurant without so much as a backward glance.

*

Furious enough to drive to base and drag a comatose man out of bed, subsequently beating a confession out of him, Max was halfway to the UCC's hub of operations before she settled down enough to make rational decisions again. Slamming on the brakes, she banged some of her frustration out against the innocent steering wheel. Then she turned the SUV around and drove back to city limits.

Arriving at Priest's townhouse, she stripped out of her borrowed clothing, popped a valium, and ran a hot bath. Recruiting the calming powers of lavender, rose, and frankincense, Max filled the tub with essential oils because, in her mind, killing the lieutenant colonel wasn't officially off the agenda yet.

He was lying. He had to be. What her father said about Priest—it couldn't be true. *This entire time, Priest was faking his feelings.*

No.

Max refused to believe it. At the very least, Priest deserved the benefit of the doubt. She owed him that much.

But now she really couldn't ignore the troubling conversation with Jensen at Gents & Belles. According to her friend, Priest's mind was literally under the control of the UCC, and he didn't have a final say over his own actions. As much as Max hated to consider it, Jensen's claims only supported what her father said at Luca's.

Ugh.

Sliding toward the foot of the garden tub, she submerged herself completely, letting the waters surge over her as if the troubles could be washed away. Beneath five inches of water, she felt the valium kick in, relaxing her muscles and slowing chaotic thoughts. Though her worries remained, Max found herself feeling a lot less frantic about them. But as the Universe would have it, fortune wasn't quite done dealing her a shitty night because through the water's surface, Max got a distorted glimpse of a face looming above her.

She froze, considering her options.

Prior to the valium taking effect, Max had been in a terribly foul mood—practically hankering for a fight. She still halfway wanted to launch herself from the tub now and get one. Let the chips fall where they may. Or she could sit up slowly and assess the situation, see what kind of pervy asshole was brave enough to break into Priest's home and barge in on a lady while she took a bath.

Gripping the sides of the tub, Max decided on a sort of compromise between the two, but once out of the water, her skin encountered what was beginning to be a familiar feeling. The atmospheric vibrations came as a gentle hum that urged the rest of her body to come forth. Max didn't resist. Breaching the water's surface in one fluid motion, she came face-to-face with the golden-eyed creature.

It smiled. "Hello, sister."

Max carefully raked the water away from her eyes with one hand, using both arms to shield her breasts from view. "Why do you keep calling me that?"

"Because we're family," he answered, bearing a wounded expression.

"I'm guessing you know my mother," Max said, thinking it was a small leap, but also the only scenario that made sense.

"I do," he said simply.

"Please tell me about her. Who is she? What's she like? Where's she from?"

"In time, Maxima. In time, I will tell you these things. For now, we must discuss a separate matter."

"And what's that?"

"You must be careful, sister."

"Yeah." She shrugged. "People keep telling me that. So, what's your reason?"

"Your eye looks far beyond what the human part of you was ever meant to see, causing great pain to you. When I sent my pet to collect something, you intervened. Furthermore, you have claimed what was meant to be my prize as your own."

"Your pet?" Max frowned in puzzlement. "Do you mean the saurummut?"

The creature nodded. Despite his allegations of theft, he appeared pleased.

"You wanted Priest's heart," she said after the creature remained silent.

"Clever girl." He stood, pacing away from the tub and then back. "I only wanted to make him my servant, but you—dear sister, you have created something so much more wonderful." He smiled again. "And forbidden."

Kneeling next to the tub, he raised his hand slowly, while watching her reaction. Max didn't flinch away as reached for her, endured the odd chill when his finger touched her skin and trailed across her bare shoulder.

"This is why you must be careful, sister."

Max shook her head. "I don't understand."

"Oh but you will. For now, it is beyond you."

His finger continued to move, wicking away several wet droplets from her body, causing her to shudder. The creature's eyes lifted to hers with a curious gaze. "Do I frighten you?"

"No," she answered quickly, but it was the truth.

"Then there is no need to for you to hide within these walls, under the protection of such vigilant guardians. Return to your home if you wish."

"I can't do that," Max said carefully, hesitant to make the connection between her fear of him and a good reason to go back to her apartment. She needed to be sure. "My boss was murdered a few days ago, and the fucking nutcase who did it left his head on top of my comforter."

"Ah." He finally slid his hand away from her body, letting it dangle in the cooling bathwater. "Forgive the dramatics. I only desired to set certain things in motion."

"Oh." She swallowed. "Why?"

Anger creased the creature's expression. "Because I am not the only one who watches you." He turned away, listening intently to something in the distant night. "I'm afraid our time has grown short, sister. We will meet again."

Max licked her lips. There were far too many questions. "But what are you? What is your name?"

"We are gods," he breathed. Then his voice dropped to a terse whisper. "Or are we monsters?" An odd smile crept onto his face. "Soon, sister."

"Wait!" Max called out, as he started to vanish. "Please wait!"

But it was futile. The creature was gone.

Sixteen

The next morning, Max couldn't think straight enough to attempt functioning at the agency. She started to leave the townhouse but found the gift bag her father had given her at dinner sitting on the front stoop. Max retrieved the bag but tossed it on the kitchen counter unopened. Then she headed straight to base, needing to see Priest—to be near him. Even if he was unconscious, maybe being next to him could help quell the storm of conflicted emotions currently raging inside of her. Or possibly, by some miracle, Priest would be conscious and talking. Then Max could grill him for some sorely needed answers.

Marching up the infirmary steps and straight to the restricted area of the ninth level, Max moved with resolute strides that practically dared anyone to make trouble. The guards on duty didn't look familiar, but there was little time to wonder whether they were friend or foe. According to her watch, Priest had less than twenty-four hours to regain consciousness and prove to command that he was still a viable, controllable asset. Thinking these could have been her final moments on Earth with Priest, Max wasn't about to let anyone stand in the way of that.

Somewhat taken aback when the team of operators allowed her to enter Priest's room without so much as a whisper of explanation or a sideways glance, Max was even more stunned to find his bed empty and the room stripped bare. No beeping machinery. No hospital linens. Just a metal bed frame and bleak grey walls.

Feeling as if the world were closing in around her, Max took two steps backward. Her mind reeled. It was hard to breathe. Whirling around, Max half-staggered, half-lunged toward the door, barely able to see past her rage or grief.

No. He should have more time. The doctor gave him thirty-six hours.

Zeroing in on the guards, Max went straight for the largest one—over six feet tall and at least seventy pounds heavier than her—and grabbed him by the collar, slamming him backward with a force that cracked the drywall. Hearing three fully-automatic weapons snap into position, she took the stunned guard by the throat and wrestled him so his armored body shielded her from the imminent gunfire of his fellow comrades. Max wasn't leaving until she found Priest...or had revenge.

"Where is he?" she demanded, barely recognizing her own voice through the snarling undercurrent of malice.

"Max?!" an unmistakable voice called in disbelief, overlapping with Dutch's awed murmur, "Well, I'll be damned."

Cautiously turning toward the sound of her name, she looked down the hallway, wanting desperately for her eyes to confirm it. Priest was alive. He was about fifty feet away, barely standing straight and wearing the typical infirmary garb—light blue sweatpants and a shirt to match. Dutch stood behind him, watching Max with an odd expression, with his hands resting on an empty wheelchair.

"Max, it's okay." Priest took a couple of steps forward, wavering unsteadily as he did so. His sapphire eyes widened with increasing distress as they assessed the unfolding situation. "Stand down." When no one moved, Priest repeated the command more firmly. "Stand down," he barked.

The guard held hostage by Max flinched. When she tightened her grip, he didn't move again, but the other three shifted uncertainly. Gradually, each of their gazes flickered to Priest and then back to Max.

One of them finally spoke. "Sir, is that order intended for Agent Masters?"

Instead of answering, Priest dropped his head, shaking it as if to clear some wayward thought. Max yearned to go to him, but her predicament remained far too volatile for her to risk taking a single step beyond the safety of cover.

Frowning, Dutch solved the dilemma. "First Sergeant Preesti is talking to you, shithead. Now you've got three seconds before I take that gun away and shove it up your government ass."

His threat was enough to satisfy any lingering doubt about the veracity of Priest's order. Nodding to his fellow unit members, the guard lowered his weapon. The others quickly followed suit. Then they clicked their heels together and stood at attention, alert for further instruction. Max released the final guard, and he too pulled himself up as straight as possible, chin tilted up, eyes forward.

Max didn't waste another second. Running to Priest, she threw herself into his waiting arms and he pulled her close, kissing her hair and forehead, sighing softly. Max buried her face into his shoulder, nearly choking on sobs of relief.

"I thought—"

"Doctor Thorne insisted on running some tests. I was downstairs getting a CT scan."

"But your room—"

"Something happened to the ventilation in there. They moved me across the hall."

"Oh," Max said simply and held him tighter.

Priest grunted, stiffening slightly, and she jerked away. "Shit. I'm sorry."

"It's okay," he said. Wincing, he clutched his side with one hand.

Relief passed, Max frowned with concern. "You should be in bed," she urged gently.

Dutch considered Priest with a wary eye. "A few moments ago, he couldn't stand up straight. Now he's jumping out of moving wheelchairs and barking orders. I think he's doing better. Still," he said, placing a hand on Priest's shoulder, "Have a seat and I'll take you back to your room."

Priest shrugged Dutch's hand off. "I can walk."

"Suit yourself. But let your girlfriend break your fall this time."

Glaring stonily at Dutch, Priest took three dogged steps before slouching into Max. Luckily, her arm was still around him, so she caught his weight easily and helped him the rest of the way. None of the guards made eye contact as they passed. Once Priest and Max were inside, Dutch parked the wheelchair against the wall and tucked both hands into his pockets.

"Though I'd love to stay and watch, I'll be a gentleman and give you two your privacy." He winked. "But don't worry, sweetcheeks. I won't go far."

Max rolled her eyes as he left the room. "He's not nearly as bad as I thought he was, but he's still pretty awful."

"Project Washington didn't grow diplomats, Max. They created soldiers."

"Then why aren't you so horrible?"

"I dunno." Priest eased himself down onto the edge of a very thin and uncomfortable-looking mattress. "Maybe I just grew on you."

Seeing him struggle to lift his legs, Max quickly moved to help. "I'm glad you're not dead, Priest, but honestly, if you were feeling better, I'd probably be beating you senseless."

His expression took on a note of distress. "Tell me what I did first."

"I talked to my father."

Priest's jaw set in a firm line. His gaze slid away from hers. "I think I know what this is about, and I can explain. But please, not here."

Max swallowed the lump in her throat. *He can't even deny it.* "If you know what this is about, then you know that what you're asking is a lot."

"It is, Max. I'm sorry about that."

Max chewed her lip. "How do I know that I can trust you, Priest? After everything?" *That's right*, she thought, closing her eyes with a blend of regret and shame. *After everything.*

"You shouldn't trust anyone. But you can trust what I feel for you."

"Which is what, exactly?" she asked, daring to push.

Priest blinked. "I love you, Maxima."

"Right." Sniffing, Max turned her back on him. She couldn't be a rational person when faced with that stare.

"Max, promise me that you won't do anything crazy or stupid until I get out of here. Tell me that you will wait for me. That you will at least give me a chance to explain."

She didn't answer, but focused on steadying her breathing, inhaling and exhaling at a slow, even pace. When tears leaked from her eyes, Max hurriedly wiped them away.

"Max?"

Oh hell.

"Max, please."

She closed her eyes. *This man will be my undoing.*

Sighing, Max returned to his bedside. Placing one knee on the paper-thin mattress, she hoisted herself up and sat astride him, purposefully meeting his radioactive eyes. Formerly pure blue, now flecks of silver danced and moved about within his irises as if they were alive. *That's odd,* she thought. And then she kissed him, because it was Priest and it was all she had thought about since seeing him in the hallway. His lips molded to hers, his skin cool and warm all at once. Given his current condition, he held her with surprising strength, his touch urgent and possessive as he pulled her closer, deepening the kiss, increasing the heat between them. His hands slid to her hips and stroked her ass, making her body respond, conjuring a familiar ache within her loins. But when Priest started to rise from the bed, Max's reaction was immediate. Grabbing him by the shoulders, she pushed him down firmly, forcing him back onto the pillows. That only served to intensify the hunger in his silver-speckled stare. Her own gaze shifted to the growing bulge in the front of his hospital-issued pants. Priest could barely walk but was ready for sex. Inwardly, Max rolled her eyes. *He'd rip his stitches out in two seconds.*

Carefully easing his shirt up from his waist, she made a study of the heavy bandages nearly covering his entire left side and part of his chest. A new marking—one Max didn't recognize stood out against the older, darker tattoos. Shimmering and silver-colored, it appeared to be a sort of cross, but was topped with a loop instead of ending with a regular straight arm. Max had seen the symbol before, many times. However, she couldn't recall the name of it or its significance and wondered why Priest would get branded with such a thing. It was nothing like his other tattoos.

Pushing her musings aside, Max brought her thoughts back to the task at hand, summoning her most teasing smile as she lowered her mouth to his chest and planted a series of gentle kisses across his tanned and inked skin. He trembled at her touch, and Max wished wholeheartedly he were in better shape. *But since he's not…*

With a resigned sigh, she kissed him one final time and lowered his shirt. "I love you too, Harrison. However," she added quickly, hoping to stave off the hope-fueled idiotic grin suddenly plastered across his face. "I'm still going to kick your ass once you get out of here. But I will wait for you, Priest. I'll wait."

THE END

OTHER WORKS

Dark Siren
Banewolf (Dark Siren #2)
Blood Chained (Darke Siren #3)
Primed Son (Dark Siren #4)

Love, Alchemy

(Coming Soon)
Love, Immortal

EDEN ASHLEY

Wordsmith. Wanderer.

Daydreamer. Night thinker.

Hopeless romantic with a

cynical mind.

For news on Upcoming books, join me on Facebook:

https://www.facebook.com/EdenAshleyAuthor

Instagram:

https://www.instagram.com/carpe.el.noche/

Twitter:

https://twitter.com/Eden_byNite

Comments, questions, thoughts, suggestions? I love to hear them all!

edenashleyromance@outlook.com